Benjamin put her hand on his arm and pulled her away.

"I have a very special friend I'd like you to meet, cousin." He pulled her toward Jared. "Jared Stuart, please meet my cousin, Amelia Montgomery."

"It's you." Her eyes, so deep, so mysterious, shone in the light of the candles. "I never got to say good-bye."

"You two know each other?" Benjamin's shocked gaze met Jared's sheepish one. "Have you been keeping secrets from me?"

"We rode the train together, but we were never properly introduced." Jared raised his spectacles to the bridge of his nose. "Luke Talbot made sure of that."

DIANE ASHLEY, a "town girl" born and raised in Mississippi, has worked more than twenty years for the House of Representatives. She rediscovered a thirst for writing, was led to a class taught by Aaron McCarver, and became a founding member of the Bards of Faith. Visit her at www.bardsoffaith.homestead.com

AARON MCCARVER is a transplanted Mississippian who was raised in the mountains near Dunlap, Tennessee. He loves his jobs of teaching at two Christian colleges and editing for Barbour Publishing. A member of ACFW, he is coauthor with Gilbert Morris of the bestselling series, The Spirit of Appalachia.

Books by Diane Ashley and Aaron McCarver

HEARTSONG PRESENTS
HP860—Under the Tulip Poplar
HP879—A Bouquet for Iris

The Mockingbird's Call

Diane Ashley and Aaron McCarver

Heartsong Presents

From Aaron: To my great-niece, Hailey Brewer. Your precious life is just beginning. May you come to share that wonderful relationship with your heavenly Father and follow His call in all you do. Always know I love you dearly.

From Diane: To the employees of the Mississippi House of Representatives, my second family. Thanks for reading my stories and for encouraging me all these years. It's an honor to work with all of you.

A note from the Authors:
We love to hear from our readers! You may correspond with us by writing:

Diane Ashley and Aaron McCarver
Author Relations
PO Box 721
Uhrichsville, OH 44683

ISBN 978-1-60260-769-9

THE MOCKINGBIRD'S CALL

All scripture quotations are taken from the King James Version of the Bible.

All of the characters and events in this book are fictitious. Any resemblance to actual persons, living or dead, or to actual events is purely coincidental.

Our mission is to publish and distribute inspirational products offering exceptional value and biblical encouragement to the masses.

PRINTED IN THE U.S.A.

one

Nashville, Tennessee
March 1861

"But I don't want to go to Virginia." Jared Stuart's jaw clenched, and he looked at his dinner plate, ignoring the creep of his spectacles down the bridge of his nose. His stomach churned, but not because of the food in front of his blurred gaze. It was his rebellious words that made him ill. He knew his parents planned for him to attend William and Mary, the school where Pa had studied law thirty years ago.

Jared's words seemed to echo from wall to wall of the well-appointed dining room. He felt a cold hand steal into his own beneath the cover of Great-Aunt Dolly's imported tablecloth. Victoria, the sister who was only a year his senior, knew of his wish to attend East Tennessee University in Knoxville. She had been his sympathetic confidante, her tender heart torn between supporting his desire to attend a small school and their parents' stated plan to send him to William and Mary.

"I don't understand why you don't want to go there." Adam Stuart's voice was not loud, but Jared could feel the frustration behind each word. "You know it's the alma mater of many of our country's founding fathers. Your own family has a history there. Your mother and I have all the connections it would take to ensure your success—"

"That's just it, Pa." Jared looked up from his plate. He could see the flecks of green in his father's brown eyes, a sign of banked anger. Resentment rose up and pressed against his throat. "I want to succeed on my own merits, not because I'm your son or Grandpa Landon's grandson."

"Going to William and Mary won't prohibit that."

"Adam." Iris Stuart's voice was barely a whisper. She shook her head slightly at her husband, and a curl sprang from her coiffure. She brushed it back with one finger. "Not now. We can talk about this later."

Great-Aunt Dolly, imperious in her black bombazine dress and her position at the head of the table, cleared her throat. "Well, I don't see what all of the rumpus is about." She lifted a wrinkled hand to her mouth and coughed for a moment before continuing. "Young people will always insist on their own ways in things." She pointed an arthritic finger at his ma. "Why I remember when the boy's grandma and I went all the way to New Orleans in the middle of a war just so she could see your pa. Didn't take Rebekah long to convince her parents to let her have her way."

"That's a different matter," Adam Stuart protested.

Great-Aunt Dolly shrugged a shoulder and looked at Jared. "You're a grown man now, and you have a good head on your shoulders. Doesn't matter to me if you want to go to school in Williamsburg, Knoxville, or even Schenectady. All you have to do is say so. I'll make sure you have the money."

"That's very generous of you, Aunt Dolly." Ma folded her napkin and laid it on the table next to her dinner plate. "But I'm sure Adam and I can afford to send our only son to college."

Jared pushed his spectacles up on his nose, bringing Pa's glare into focus. He refused to drop his gaze this time. He noticed the gray sideburns that framed his father's face and wondered how Pa always managed to look so distinguished. His clothes were always neatly pressed, his necktie folded into crisp lines, and his shoes brightly polished. No matter the situation, the great Adam Stuart was always in control. He might have been about to make a speech at the capitol instead of sitting at the dinner table with his family.

A part of Jared wanted to acquiesce to Pa's wish, but he could not compromise on this. He had prayed about his decision before sending an application to East Tennessee University last month, prayed for a sign like Gideon's fleece, something so clear he couldn't mistake it. And last week he'd gotten his answer in a letter of enthusiastic acceptance sent by the college in Knoxville. Now all he had to do was convince his parents.

What would he do if he couldn't convince them? Take Great-Aunt Dolly's money? He hoped it wouldn't come to that. He turned his attention to the diminutive little lady. "Thank you for your offer, but I have a little money saved. It's enough to pay for a term."

Pa tossed his napkin on the table and shoved his chair back. "We'll talk about this later." He helped Great-Aunt Dolly roll her wheelchair back and out of the dining room.

Victoria, her wide brown eyes shiny with unshed tears, squeezed Jared's hand and leaned toward him. "I'm very proud of you for telling them the truth."

"I'm glad someone is." Jared felt the tension seeping from his chest, leaving a regretful heart in its wake. He pulled his hand from his sister's and stood up.

How he wished he could walk out the door, get on a horse, and be transported to the campus in Knoxville. Instead, he helped his mother rise from her seat. Her eyes, an older version of Victoria's, searched his face. Light from the candelabra caught a few strands of gray that were beginning to appear in the ringlets around her temples. He and Ma were nearly the same height, and he had been told that they favored each other strongly, even though his coloring—light brown hair and hazel eyes—came from his pa. "I'm sorry."

She patted his cheek before smoothing one of the loose curls, so like her own, that sprang from his head. "You're a good son, Jared. Your pa and I know that." She sighed. "And I am not unhappy to think of you in Knoxville instead of Williamsburg. There is so much unrest these days."

"Pa should be glad you don't want to join the militia," Victoria chimed in. She was such a sweet, unpretentious young woman. He often forgot he was her junior.

Jared offered both elbows to escort the ladies of his family to the parlor for coffee and dessert. "I'm not going to change my mind, Ma."

"I know that, son." She smiled at him. "You are too much like your father in that respect. Once he's plotted his course, few people can convince him to reconsider."

"You can." Jared straightened his shoulders, wishing they were as wide as his father's. It seemed he'd spent his whole life measuring himself against Adam Stuart. And he'd always come up lacking.

The list of his father's successes was as long as the Cumberland River. After marrying Jared's ma, Adam Stuart had spent more than two decades in the southeastern corner of Tennessee, fighting for Indians' rights in the courtroom, and he won more often than he lost. Then he and Ma decided to take their fight to the halls of state government. They'd moved in with Great-Aunt Dolly and Great-Uncle Mac several years ago, expecting to stay for a few weeks while the legislature was in session. But those weeks grew into months. Ma started teaching at the Indian school on the west side of town, even though few Cherokee lived in

Nashville since President Jackson had ordered their removal decades earlier. Jared's older sister, Agnes, fell in love and married a man from Nashville. Then Great-Uncle Mac died and Great-Aunt Dolly's health began to fail. So his parents made the decision to stay in Nashville to care for her.

They'd been in Nashville now for more than four years. Agnes had become one of the leading matrons of the city, and Pa's law practice was thriving as he became the voice for his clients, bringing their issues to the notice of the Tennessee legislature. Even Victoria had gotten past her slight gawkiness and tendency toward diffidence. There always seemed to be a suitor or two lounging in the parlor, hoping to take her on a picnic or carriage ride. Jared had no doubt she would soon accept an offer of marriage from one of them and join her older sister in Nashville's highest social circles. Everyone seemed to be succeeding. . .everyone but him.

Jared missed the quiet days of life back home in Chattanooga. He missed the tree-strewn mountains and wide plateaus. He didn't like the hustle and bustle that seemed to surround his family here. Nor did he want to follow in his father's footsteps. The idea of testifying to a bunch of hot-tempered politicians made him physically ill. All he wanted was to go to college, maybe find a friend or two, and study.

Was that too much to ask?

❧

Jared caressed the paisley cover of the slender book of poetry he held. How would it feel to see his own name printed there? Excitement raced through him. His finger traced the name—Henry Wadsworth Longfellow—while he imagined sending his own work to a publisher and having it accepted. Would it be as soul stirring as this volume entitled *Poems on Slavery* or as heartbreaking as Harriet Beecher Stowe's novel?

Could he write anything as effective as either publication in describing the horror and tragedy of slavery? Or would he find some other school of thought to explore in the manner of Socrates or Plato?

"Jared, where are you?" His sister's voice broke through Jared's reverie.

He glanced at the ornate longcase clock standing in a corner of the library. It wasn't time for dinner yet. What could Victoria want? Why couldn't his family allow him a little time of quiet to read? He heaved a sigh and arose from the deep leather chair that had once belonged to Great-Uncle Mac. He reached the door just as his sister pulled it open.

She clucked her tongue. "I should have known you'd be here. Don't you ever get tired of reading?"

"How can I?" He swept an arm back to indicate the room behind him. "There's so much in Great-Aunt Dolly's library I haven't read. So much to learn."

"Of course there is."

Her sigh indicated a lack of understanding. But then, most of his family did not share his addiction to the written word. They'd rather attend a play than spend time reading. He was the bookish one. Maybe it was because of his spectacles. Maybe it was because he understood better than they the importance of books, poems, and biographies. "Were you looking for me?"

"Oh, yes." Her cheeks reddened slightly. "Pa has someone he wants you to meet. They're in the drawing room." She turned and led the way down the hall.

Jared wanted to groan. Probably another politician, someone to remind him how popular and important his father was. Well, he would give the man five polite minutes and then slip away to the library once more. He knew from experience he would not be missed.

His father pushed away from the mantel as Jared entered the room. "I have brought someone home who is eager to meet you, son." He nodded to the man seated next to his mother. "William, this is my son, Jared."

Jared noticed the stranger's conservative suit, blond hair, and deep-set green eyes that seemed to be lit from within. A wide, attractive smile graced the man's face as he stood and held out his right hand. "I have heard much about you from your father, young man."

"Pleased to meet you, sir," Jared mumbled, uncomfortable as always when he found himself the center of attention.

"Your father tells me you are interested in attending my college this fall."

What new stratagem had his father concocted in his efforts to force Jared to attend William and Mary? He tossed a long-suffering glance toward his sister.

She shook her head slightly in response. Was she trying to warn him now when it was too late? Why couldn't she have said something before? Her betrayal was like a slap.

He returned his attention to the man standing before him. "I'm afraid you are mistaken, sir—"

His mother started coughing so loudly that Jared stopped in midsentence.

He glanced at her, and her eyes were full of meaning, but he had no idea what message she was trying to convey.

A look of confusion entered the shorter man's expression. "You no longer want to attend East Tennessee University?"

"East Tennessee?" He looked at his father, who was smiling broadly and nodding. He turned back to the visitor. "No, sir . . .I mean, yes, sir. . .I mean. . ." His words faltered to a halt. How could he express all the thoughts running through his mind at this moment?

"You'll have to forgive my son's confusion." Adam chuckled. "We have been having a long-running discussion on the subject, and I have always encouraged him to attend my alma mater." He turned to Jared. "I met Reverend Carnes at the capitol today. He has come down from Knoxville to talk to the legislature about increased funding while they are in special session."

Reverend Carnes? Reverend William Carnes, the president of East Tennessee University? Excitement bubbled up in Jared's chest. His father had brought the president of East Tennessee University home with him! This must mean Pa had given up his desire to make Jared attend William and Mary. He was acceding to Jared's wishes. Now his mother's silent message became clear. She and his sister had been trying to keep him from making a fool of himself.

Reverend Carnes's wide smile caused a dimple to appear in his right cheek. "Your father was kind enough to share his insights on which of our elected officials might be receptive to my appeal. After the hearing, he introduced me to several of the senators and representatives. Because of his expertise, I have high hopes that East Tennessee University will benefit from my trip to Nashville."

Their explanations had given Jared the respite he needed to collect his thoughts. "I'm glad to hear that. No one in the state is more knowledgeable than my pa when it comes to the inner workings of the Tennessee legislature."

Reverend Carnes reclaimed his seat and accepted a cup of tea from Jared's mother. "I have to agree."

Jared sat down as well; all thoughts of slipping away were forgotten. Over the next hour, he grilled the university president on all the particulars of the campus. He was pleased to have his parents made aware of the outstanding moral and educational goals of the school. From the compulsory attendance at chapel twice daily to the challenging curriculum of the faculty, it was obvious that East Tennessee demanded the best from its students. And then there were the literary societies and even a literary magazine. It was the perfect place for an aspiring writer.

By the time Reverend Carnes took his leave, Jared was practically floating in the clouds. As soon as the college president left, he approached his father and thrust out his right hand. "Thank you, Pa."

His father grasped his hand and pulled Jared into an embrace. "I love you, son. Don't ever doubt that your ma and I have your best interests at heart. We believe in you."

He felt somewhat awkward as he and his father had not embraced since Jared had left his childhood behind. But this was a special day—one that Jared knew he would always remember. Emotion tried to overwhelm him, but he choked it back. "I won't let you down."

two

Montgomery Plantation, outside Nashville

Amelia Montgomery's skirt threatened to halt her progress as she followed her mother through the slave cabin's tiny doorway. She reached down with impatient hands and compressed the voluminous material so she could successfully negotiate the narrow entrance. While hoops allowed a ladylike sway in one's progress, they could often be quite cumbersome.

What she saw inside took her breath away and filled her tender heart with sorrow. One rickety table stood in the center of the room with three tree stumps placed around it, apparently serving as chairs. A few tattered blankets were laid out on the dirt floor of the cabin. On one of the blankets lay a very young girl, probably only five or six years old, who was alternately coughing and moaning, obviously in the grip of some dangerous disease. A shallow bowl filled with water and a wad of rags indicated that the only other occupant of the one-room cabin, probably the mother of the little girl, had been bathing her forehead with cool water. Now she stood to one side as Amelia's mother set her basket on the table and drew off her gloves.

"Esau told me your little girl was sick, Nelly." Amelia's mother referred to the butler at the big house. She took an apron from her basket. "Amelia and I have brought some medicine for you to use that should have her feeling better in no time."

"Thank you, Mrs. Montgomery, Miss Amelia." The older

woman's face was so dark that Amelia could barely make out her expression in the dim cabin.

It was a shame they could not leave the door open to let light inside, but it was much too cold and the little girl was much too sick.

"What do you want me to do, Mama?"

Amelia's mother sank to the ground next to the blanket and placed her hand on the child's forehead. "I need you to measure out a spoonful of the butterfly root tea we brought. If we can get her to drink some, it will help with the fever and coughing."

Amelia opened the medicine bag her mother had helped her prepare, withdrew the warm bottle, and uncorked it, wrinkling her nose at the pungent smell.

Mrs. Montgomery took the spoon from her as soon as Amelia filled it. She coaxed the child to open her mouth and tipped the spoon against her lips. The poor thing was so weak and sick she didn't even react to what Amelia imagined was a very bitter dose.

She took the spoon back from her mother. "Another one?"

Her mother shook her head. "We don't want to give her too much." She laid the child back down on the blanket. "Hand me a towel."

Amelia drew out a pair of snowy white cotton towels and watched as her mother arranged them under the little girl's head. "If you will keep her head up like this, Nelly, she will be able to breathe more easily." She pushed herself up from the ground and dusted her hands together.

"Thank you, ma'am. I been so worried about my Sadie. She been gettin' worse since Sunday."

"And rightly so." Mrs. Montgomery took the bottle and spoon from Amelia. "It appears your child has pneumonia.

You will need to give her one spoonful of this medicine every hour until you go to sleep tonight."

Amelia's forehead wrinkled with doubt. "But, Mama, how will Nelly know when an hour has passed?"

"Don't you fret yourself, Miss Amelia. I knows how to watch the sun."

"I'm going to leave this basket with you, Nelly. There's food inside for your family since you can't work today and earn your portion. You'll need to get one of the older women to watch after her tomorrow, though, so you can get back to work. Tell her to give your girl a spoonful at a time until this bottle is empty."

The woman thanked her mother yet again for her kind Christian heart even as the child started coughing and moaning once again.

Amelia grabbed her skirts and followed her mother back outside. Cold winter air reddened her cheeks in the few steps it took for them to reach the family carriage. Once inside, she looked at her mother. "Will her child live?"

"I don't know, but we've done all we can." Her mother shivered and pulled a thick fleece blanket over her lap. "We must always take care to provide medicine and care for the slaves, Amelia. It's our Christian duty to them. And it will ensure that we'll never be troubled by a slave uprising."

Amelia nodded, but she wondered. If that had been her little girl, would she have been so thankful for a basket of food and medicine? "Can't we make their quarters warmer?"

Her mother sniffed. "They don't need warmth like we do. They are accustomed to harsher circumstances. Just as there is a danger in ignoring their needs, there is a danger in coddling them too much."

Coddling? Amelia didn't think basic comfort was coddling.

She opened her mouth to argue, but the coachman pulled up at the front steps and ended their conversation. She would remember to ask Papa later. Perhaps he would be more sympathetic to his workers' needs.

❧

Amelia pushed against the pommels of her sidesaddle to get a higher vantage point and looked all around the fields. The fall harvest had begun even though it was barely September. She could see the dark heads of the field workers as they toiled in the bright sunlight to the shouts and warnings of the overseer. She winced as the crack of a whip carried to her over the hot wind. She hoped none of Nelly's family was being punished.

In the months since she had first visited Nelly's cabin with her mother, Amelia had often dropped by to see how little Sadie was progressing. It had taken the girl a long time to recover from the pneumonia, but the cough had finally disappeared as the hot summer days grew longer. Amelia had taken Sadie gifts, trinkets really—a pan of biscuits, a handkerchief made of soft lawn, and a shift she had cut from one of her old nightgowns. She thought of the gift she brought today, eager to see a smile on little Sadie's face.

Now she glanced around to make certain no one was watching as she turned her mare's head toward the group of slave cabins her parents called the quarters. Mama and Papa would skin her if they knew what she was doing. They had strict views on which slaves she could befriend.

Tabitha, her personal maid, was an acceptable friend and confidante. Tabitha was the daughter of Esau, the butler, and Rahab, the mulatto cook. As higher-echelon slaves, Esau and Rahab had been allowed to marry and lived in much nicer accommodations than those to be found in the quarters.

She and Tabitha were very close in age, having been born only a month apart. She often pulled Tabitha into scrapes, like wading barefoot in the stream or sneaking fresh cream out to the barn cat after she delivered a litter of tiny, mewing kittens. But if they were caught, she was always quick to accept the total blame, aware that her punishment would always be lighter than that of a slave.

That was why Amelia had never brought Tabitha with her to the quarters. If Papa ever caught her friend out there, he'd probably sell her to one of the neighboring landowners. He had very strict rules about the house slaves keeping separate from the field slaves. The only time they were allowed to be in the same building together was on Sundays at church, and even then the house slaves had to sit with the family while the field slaves occupied the balcony on the second floor. Amelia didn't understand why the separation was so important, but she knew enough to be careful which of Papa's rules she broke.

The hot, dry wind chased Amelia into the quarters.

Sadie came running toward her before she even had time to dismount. "Hi, Miss Amelia." Sadie's slender legs showed beneath the hem of her shift as she skidded to a stop.

"I declare, Sadie, if you don't stop growing, that shift is going to be too short for you before winter returns."

The little girl glanced at her bare toes. "Yes, ma'am. But I can't he'p it. Ev'y night I ask Jesus to keep me short, but ev'y day when I gets up, my legs is longer."

Amelia laughed and reached out a hand to pull Sadie into the saddle behind her. "I've got a surprise for you today."

"A surprise?" Excitement made Sadie twist and turn behind her. "Where is it?"

"I left it in my saddlebag. To see it properly you and I are going to have to go to the creek."

Sadie wrapped her hands around Amelia's waist. "Is it a fishing line? I likes fish, Miss Amelia."

"No, it's not a fishing line. But I'm not going to tell you anything else until we get to the creek." She clucked to her horse.

It only took them a couple of minutes to reach the shady banks of the trickling stream. Sadie slid off the horse first, and Amelia dismounted right after her. Having secured the reins on a nearby branch, she went to her saddlebag and made a production of pulling out a little reed boat she and Tabitha had woven the day before.

Sadie's mouth opened in an O. "What is it?"

"It's a boat just like a reed boat that once hid a little baby boy in Egypt a long time ago."

"Who would hide a baby in a boat?"

Amelia pulled off her shoes and stockings and sat on the bank of the creek. "A long time ago, a big king reigned in Egypt, and he was a very bad man. He had lots of Hebrew slaves, so many that he decided to kill all the little boy slaves so he wouldn't lose his power over them."

Sadie sat down beside her and dangled her feet in the water.

Amelia handed her the little boat to play with. "One day, a Hebrew woman had a baby boy. She loved him so much that she hid him in a boat to keep the bad king from killing him."

"Was he in the boat a long time?"

"No." Amelia shook her head. "The king's daughter found him, and she loved him like her own little boy. She brought him back to her home and named him Moses. When he was a grown man, he used his power to free his people."

"That's a nice story, Miss Amelia." Sadie moved the little boat back and forth in the water. "I wish I had a Moses to free my family."

"Amelia Montgomery!" Her father's angry voice startled Amelia. How had he managed to find them, and how long had he been listening?

She turned to face his wrath, praying that he would not take his anger out on the little girl beside her.

Her father's face reminded her of a thundercloud. His eyes blazed, and his teeth were gritted. He pulled his hat off and slapped it against his leg. She watched the dust billow from his pants leg and swirl around in the dry air. Next to him stood one of the overseers, a heavy-jowled man with mean little eyes and a hard mouth.

"Papa, I'm sorry."

"I don't want to hear a word from you, Amelia. Get back home and await me in my study." He turned to the overseer. "Obviously, this slave has too much time on her hands. Take her out to the fields. She can start to earn her keep."

"Papa, no." Amelia put her hand out and stepped toward him. "Please don't."

"This time you've gone too far, Amelia, sowing discord with your tales of slave uprisings." He grabbed her arm and dragged her to her mare, tossing Amelia in the saddle and slapping her mount's flank. As she grabbed for the reins to keep from tumbling to the ground, Amelia heard Sadie screaming behind her.

All the way home, Amelia prayed for God to intervene. She'd never meant to encourage rebellion. It had only been a Bible story. Tears of remorse made hot tracks down her cheeks as she reached the house. She dismounted and handed her horse to a stable boy before dragging her reluctant feet to Papa's study.

Inside the stuffy room, time slowed to a crawl. The bright afternoon faded to dusk, and still Papa did not come. Just when she thought he'd forgotten her, the door opened, and he stomped in.

Amelia stood up, uncertain what to say. She watched as he went to the far side of his large chestnut desk and dropped into his chair, leaning back and gazing at the ceiling as if searching for the right words. Then he looked at her, his eyes colder than she'd ever seen them. She opened her mouth to speak, but he held up his hand.

"I've obviously pampered you too much, daughter. I learned today that you do not understand the least thing about our livelihood, our very existence. I might be able to make allowances for some young woman who lived far away and knew nothing of plantation life, but I cannot abide treachery within my own household."

"But, Papa—"

"No, not a single word will I entertain from you, Amelia Montgomery. Your behavior this afternoon was inexcusable. I have tolerated your liberal ideas for far too long, thinking you would grow out of your ridiculous beliefs once you understood the way of the world. But I was mistaken. I cannot and will not tolerate your rebellious ways any longer. I've made arrangements for you to travel to Knoxville to stay with your aunt and uncle for a year or so. They have offered to have you visit several times, but your mother and I always turned them down. We didn't know we were raising such an ungrateful, spoiled child."

"What about Sadie?" Amelia slipped the question in as her father took a breath.

"She's no concern of yours any longer." He pushed himself out of his chair and strode toward her, anger mottling his face. "You're going to be too busy getting ready for your journey."

Fresh tears flowed down her cheeks. Did her father hate her? He must. Why else would he send her away to live with people she barely knew? And what about her mother? What did she have to say about all this? Would she intervene on her daughter's behalf, or would she agree to the banishment?

"I spent the afternoon making plans with Gregory Talbot." Her father had turned back to her, his expression as unyielding as his words. "Luke wants to join up with the army, but his father has convinced him to return to school in Knoxville for his final year. He'll be leaving on Friday. His father and I agreed that Luke will escort you to your aunt and uncle's home. I will go to Nashville tomorrow to make the arrangements for your trip and to telegraph your aunt and uncle about your impending visit. I've decided you may take your maid, Tabitha, to keep you company and protect your reputation since you'll have to overnight in Chattanooga. You will board the train in Nashville two days hence. I trust that will allow you sufficient time to pack your things and say good-bye to your mother." He sat down at his desk once again and straightened a stack of papers on its surface. "I did not inform the Talbots of your views and recent indiscretion, and I expect you to keep the information quiet, also. You're excused."

Amelia put a hand over her mouth to stifle her sobs and stumbled out of the room. In the space of one afternoon, everything had changed so much that she wondered if she would ever be allowed to come home again.

three

Amelia was already tired by the time they reached the train station in Nashville, even though it was not yet midday. She, Luke Talbot, and her maid, Tabitha, had departed before daylight to ensure their timely arrival. The chaos they encountered at the crowded depot was overwhelming and frightening for someone who rarely ventured from her parents' plantation. She was glad to have the escort of an experienced traveler. Luke had made the trip to Knoxville several times and knew exactly where they should go.

Feeling like a country bumpkin, Amelia gazed on the large brick building that was the station house. It was an odd-looking building with crenulated towers and roof and two enormous arched doorways that made her feel tiny in comparison.

Off in the distance at the very top of a hill, she saw the newly completed state capitol, with its soaring central tower and tall white columns. The sight made her proud to be from the state of Tennessee. If only the North and the South could put aside their differences and come to some kind of agreement. She wished she was smart enough to figure out a solution to eliminate the need for slave labor. The barbaric practice was tearing the country apart. No matter how long she spent in exile with her relatives, Amelia knew she would never change her mind on this topic. One day, she hoped to see all of Papa's slaves set free. But that was a problem for another day. Today, she needed to concentrate on her journey.

Train tracks ran hither and yon around the station in a dizzying patchwork. She held on to Luke's arm with one hand as he threaded his way around crowds of people and piles of luggage. Her skirt threatened to tangle around her ankles, and Amelia wished she might have worn her hoops instead of five layers of petticoats. But hoops, although cooler, would be impractical once she was seated on one of the benches in the passenger car. She glanced over her shoulder several times to make certain Tabitha had not gotten separated from them, reassured when encountering the smile on her slave's face. She thanked God again for Papa's decision to allow Tabitha to accompany her during her exile. No matter how many strangers she encountered over the coming year, Amelia knew she would have one friend in Knoxville—two counting Luke Talbot.

All the noise and smoke was overwhelming. Amelia was a bit worried she might lose her grasp on Luke's strong arm and vanish in the swirling, noisy crowd. She'd never seen so many people. Young men in uniform vied for space amongst soberly clad businessmen. Importunate merchants hawked everything from newspapers to blankets. Shouts and grunts filled the air as slaves loaded cargo into crowded boxcars.

The smells of overheated bodies and live animals pushed in on her and made Amelia yearn for the country and a breath of fresh air. But she might as well put that behind her. Papa had made it clear she was not to come home before this time next year. By then, he said, the fighting would be over and things would be back to normal. He also made it clear she was to learn her place while staying in Knoxville. He wanted her to set aside reading newspapers and confine herself to novels to avoid further addling her thinking. He'd warned of dire consequences if she did not learn to conform her behavior to what was expected of a Southern lady of means.

"We are nearly there." Luke pointed to a long, black car with wide windows that vaguely resembled an iron carriage. It was one in a long line of cars attached to a locomotive that belched black smoke from a tall pipe at its front.

"Praise God." Amelia felt Luke's gaze on her and looked up at him. He was such a nice man, and she had forgotten how handsome he was. He seemed so much more grown-up now, perhaps because of the years he'd spent away at college. He sported a thin mustache and neatly trimmed side whiskers that made him appear older than his twenty years. Gone was the lanky youngster she remembered from their shared childhood. Luke carried himself well, as befitted the eldest son of a wealthy planter. His well-made clothing was fashionable, from the brim of his tall black hat to the polished toes of his leather boots.

"I am looking forward to getting back to Knoxville." He patted her hand. "I know you will enjoy yourself there, Amelia. I hope to call on you often. Perhaps your uncle will allow me to escort you about town once you are settled in."

She nodded. "It will be comforting to know I have a friend nearby."

Luke smiled, showing his even, white teeth. "You may be certain of that. But I have the feeling it will not take long for someone as pretty as you to acquire a wide circle of admirers. I only hope you will still remember me then."

Amelia reached for her fan and opened it in front of her face to cover her embarrassment. She did not know how to answer Luke. If she agreed with his compliment she would appear conceited, but if she disagreed he might think she meant that she would no longer remember him as a friend once she became established. Uncertain of what to say, she decided to say nothing and pretended a sudden interest in a group of people who were standing a few feet away.

They appeared to be a family saying good-bye to a young man about her age. The older lady wore a wide spring bonnet on her head, its upturned bill decorated with a bunch of flowers and greenery. She might have stepped out of *Godey's Lady's Book*, with her pale yellow bodice and matching skirt. She leaned over and kissed the young man, making his cheeks redden. He pushed his spectacles up on his nose and turned to the tall, handsome man who must be his father. Amelia wondered if the older man was a politician. He looked distinguished enough to be the governor. She watched as the two shook hands and embraced in the awkward way of men. Then the young man turned to a pair of ladies who were either sisters or some other close relatives. They all had the same look about them—tall, attractive, and openly affectionate.

An unexpected jab of envy straightened Amelia's spine. She'd always wanted to be part of a close-knit family like the one she was watching. Her parents had not bothered to accompany their only daughter to Nashville. Where had she gone wrong? Must she compromise her beliefs to be loved by her parents? Or was she destined to always fight alone for what she believed was right? Another thought struck her. Why was she so certain she was right? Perhaps the young man she was watching was more humble than she. Or was he simply the type who blindly embraced the beliefs of his elders?

Amelia sniffed and picked up the skirt of her gown with her free hand. The bespectacled young man was probably devoid of principles and incapable of independent thought.

She was cut from different cloth. Amelia had been brought up on the Bible, and she knew right from wrong. She would not bow to her parents or anyone else who tried to convince her to abandon her principles. So what if she had to go live with strangers for a year? She was determined to make the best of the situation. All she had to do was keep herself from getting involved in political matters and concentrate on enjoying the round of parties and social events her relatives would no doubt be invited to. Then she could return home older, wiser, and more able to persuade her parents that times were changing.

After leading her to a seat in one of the passenger cars, Luke bent over Amelia. "I'm going to take Tabitha with me to make sure your luggage has been loaded. Are you comfortable?"

"Don't worry about me." Amelia put a bright smile on her face even though she didn't much like the idea of being left completely alone. Tabitha knew all of their trunks, but she could not be sent by herself lest she be picked up by a bounty hunter mistaking her for an escaping slave. "I have Mr. Dickens's book to read. I'll be fine until you return."

≈

Jared leaned out of the doorway and waved until the train turned a bend and he could no longer see his family. He stepped into the narrow space between cars and pulled off his spectacles which had unaccountably become blurry. The problem couldn't be connected to the burning sensation in his eyes. That would mean he was crying. Grown men didn't cry. Surreptitiously, he wiped the lenses clean and replaced the spectacles, looking around to see if he'd been noticed.

He opened the door in front of him just as the train lurched. Allowing the movement to push him forward, Jared passed several benches and chose one that was unoccupied.

That's when he noticed the lovely young lady sitting on the other side of the aisle from him.

She glanced in his direction before modestly returning her attention to the book in her lap. She was the most beautiful girl in the world. The quick glance she sent his direction showed eyes as blue as a summer sky. He also noticed her delicate complexion and generous, bow-shaped mouth. Although her hair was pulled up and mostly hidden under her bonnet, he could see shimmering strands around her face that reminded him of sun-drenched corn silk. She could be the subject of poetry, perhaps the fabled Helen of Troy.

The train began to pick up speed as they moved farther away from the station, seeming to race as quickly as his mind. Where was the young lady's maid? Was she traveling alone? Chivalry filled his chest and squared his shoulders. Like a knight of old he could watch over her and make sure she reached Chattanooga safely.

His imagination soared. Over the next couple of hours, Jared would gradually win her confidence and offer her his protection. If she was traveling beyond Chattanooga on this train, he would speak to the conductor about her and make certain a suitable replacement would help her reach her final destination. If by some miraculous chance she was journeying to Knoxville, he would guard her from all the dangers they might encounter. It was the least he could do. If one of his sisters found herself traveling alone in these dangerous times, he would hope some man might do the same.

He tilted his head to see what she might be reading. Perhaps that would be a good place to start a conversation. It was a fairly thick volume, so not a book of poetry. Jared craned his neck farther but could not see the title. He thought he saw her gaze slide in his direction, so Jared sat back and straightened his cravat. He didn't want to make her nervous.

After a moment, she returned her attention to her book and turned a page. From the corner of his vision he saw a red ribbon she must be using as a bookmark flutter to the floor between their seats. Jared reached down for it at the same time as the young woman, narrowly avoiding a head collision.

He plucked the ribbon from the floor and put it in her hand, noticing her dainty wrist and long fingers. "You dropped your ribbon." He nearly groaned as he heard the words. He sounded like a simpleton. Why couldn't he think of something besides the obvious to say?

"Thank you." Her smile was perfect, friendly but shy. Her fingers closed over the ribbon, and she settled back in her seat.

Say something! His mind screamed the words, but nothing came to him. His gaze lit on her book. She had partially closed it when she reached for the ribbon. He saw the title and inspiration struck. "You're reading *A Tale of Two Cities.* What do you think of it? Dickens is one of my favorite authors. I was hoping to procure a copy of that novel before leaving Nashville, but with this and that, I never quite found the time to visit the bookseller. I hope to purchase it once I reach Knoxville. If I can find someone to tell me where the bookseller is located, of course." He cringed as he realized he was babbling.

She opened her mouth to answer him but was stopped by the arrival of a broad-shouldered man who looked a year or two older, and much more debonair than Jared could ever hope to be. A brother?

"Is this man bothering you, Amelia?" The newcomer's ferocious frown raked Jared from head to foot, and Jared's hope of protecting the pretty traveler withered.

"Oh no, Luke." She reached up and put a hand on the man's arm. "I was clumsy enough to drop my bookmark, and he most kindly returned it to me."

A harrumph from Luke indicated his skepticism. "You ought not speak to strangers, Amelia, no matter the circumstances." He turned to the black woman standing quietly in the aisle. "Sit down next to your mistress, Tabitha. Perhaps between us, we can keep her out of trouble."

Jared stared straight ahead, but he could see the two women settling next to each other. The hair prickled on the back of his neck, and he looked up to see the belligerent Luke standing over him and frowning.

"Would you move over?" The man's voice was filled with exasperation.

"Oh." Jared could feel his cheeks heating up. "Of course." He grabbed the tails of his coat and scooted toward the window.

Luke's frown never disappeared, even as he sat down and pulled out his watch to check the time. If this man was Amelia's brother, he must take after another side of the family. While she was fair and delicate, he was dark, with ebony hair and eyes. His mustache and side whiskers made him appear more sophisticated than his companions. Jared stroked his own face, wishing he could grow a respectable mustache or maybe even a beard. His smooth chin, coupled with his spectacles, had caused many a new acquaintance to think he was still a boy.

"I beg your pardon, sir." Jared fingered his cravat once more. "I meant no disrespect to the lady." He wanted to explain his motives but decided to leave well enough alone when he encountered another glare from the man. Instead, he settled back against the wooden seat and gazed out the window at the passing scenery. Eventually, the rhythmic clacking of the train's wheels eased his embarrassment and lulled him into a state of somnolence.

A feminine giggle roused him, and Jared looked past the broad chest of his seatmate toward Amelia and her maid. What was the latter's name? It was something biblical. His mind searched. Tabitha! That was it. Both women had removed their bonnets during the trip, and now they sat whispering together, their heads nearly touching. It was a charming sight, straight blond tresses mixing with ebony curls. He was glad to see they were enjoying their journey. He would have liked to join their conversation, but he knew the man sitting next to him would never abide such a thing.

Jared told himself it didn't matter. She was a stranger, and he would probably never see her again once he disembarked at Chattanooga, where he would have to spend the night before catching the train to Knoxville. But he still felt drawn to her, wanting to know where she lived, where she was going, what her dreams and aspirations were. Was his inclination a nudge from God? Or did it come from his own, more shallow desire?

ஐ

The shrill blow of the locomotive's whistle pulled Amelia's attention away from the trials of Lucie Manette and Charles Darnay in the compelling novel she was reading.

Tabitha had fallen asleep next to her, but now she awakened with a start. "Is something wrong?"

Amelia glanced out of the window and realized the day was drawing to a close. The sun had fallen below the western ridge of tree-covered hills, casting the valley they were traveling through into darkness. Smoky gray fog rose up and blurred the trees on the upward slopes of the hills surrounding them. She craned her neck but could find no evidence of a threat. "Everything seems fine."

The train whistle blew once more, and Luke leaned toward them. "We're about to reach the end of this leg of our journey. As soon as we climb out of this valley, you'll be able to see Chattanooga."

"And we'll spend the night there?"

Luke nodded. "We'll be staying at a boardinghouse where I've overnighted several times before. I think you'll find it to your liking."

"Look at that." Tabitha pointed out the window.

While they had been talking, the train had chugged its way up to the peak, and the valley was spread out below them. Amelia caught her breath. The river at the bottom of the valley looked like an ebony ribbon, its surface gleaming as it caught the light of the rising moon. The curve of the river reminded her of a bird's nest with the town of Chattanooga serving as its hatchling. "It's beautiful. So different from Nashville." She watched spellbound as the train made its descent into the valley, slowing as it reached the station.

When the car stopped, she was glad to lean on Luke's arm once more. It was so nice to have a knowledgeable guide. Over the years, her parents had encouraged her to consider him as an eligible candidate for marriage, but somehow she'd never been able to think of him that way. She supposed it was all the time they'd spent together growing up. Luke had always acted more like a brother than a suitor.

But now she was having second thoughts. Luke was capable, handsome, and smart. Perhaps she should take her parents' advice. It might even help restore her to their good graces.

❧

Jared pulled on his boots and slipped out of the room just as the sun was beginning to make its presence known in the east. He left the boardinghouse and wandered through his former hometown. Chattanooga had grown in the past four years. New businesses had sprung up, and he spotted several new houses dotting the area in the curve of the Tennessee River.

He returned to his room as the town began to come to life. Seizing the opportunity for quiet reflection, he grabbed his Bible and escaped to the small garden behind the boardinghouse. The train would not depart for Knoxville for at least two hours, which left him plenty of time for prayer before he joined the other travelers for breakfast.

A feeling of peace settled on his shoulders. These were the times he'd missed while living in Nashville with Great-Aunt Dolly. He looked up at the limbs of a tree, noticing that its leaves were beginning to turn brown with the approach of winter. Although Jared knew God was everywhere, the silence and peace of these surroundings made him feel closer to his Lord than anywhere else.

He thumbed through his Bible and finally settled on the 53rd chapter of Isaiah where he read about the slaughtered lamb. Had Isaiah felt the horror of his prophecies? It must have been terrible to foresee the undeserved death of Christ. Or had Isaiah been comforted by the prophecy that ended that chapter? Jared read the words again, his finger tracing the lines. *"And he bare the sin of many, and made intercession for transgressors."* For a moment, guilt threatened to crush him. He was one of the transgressors for whom Christ had gone silently to the cross. But then he allowed the Spirit to comfort him with the knowledge that he was forgiven and that his sins had been removed and miraculously forgotten.

Jared sank to his knees, thanking God for forgiveness for the sins that had separated him from his Maker. The peace he had felt earlier flowed more strongly. He could sense the risen Christ holding out His arms for an embrace. He basked in the love and wonder of that image.

Jared had no idea how much time passed before he heard someone walking toward him. The newcomer stepped into his line of vision, and Jared's breath caught in his throat. It was her! The beauty from the train, the girl who read Dickens. "Miss Amelia!" He scrambled to his feet and brushed at the leaves that clung to his trousers. "Good morning."

She stopped as soon as she saw him, standing in a shaft of sunlight that made her hair glow. "I'm sorry. I didn't realize anyone would be out here. I came to explore the garden. From my window it appeared too inviting to ignore. I didn't mean to disturb your privacy."

"It is beautiful, isn't it?" Jared couldn't imagine any setting more breathtaking than the girl who stood facing him. He cleared his throat, his mind scurrying to find the words to tell her his thoughts.

She turned slightly away from him. "I should be getting back to my room."

"Please don't leave on my account. I was just reading from my Bible. I love coming outside and talking to God."

She turned back to him, her expression showing interest. "What scripture are you reading?"

"Isaiah, the 53rd chapter."

Her brow wrinkled. "That's a hard book for me to understand. I prefer reading the New Testament. Especially Paul's letters. They are full of so much hope."

"That's the way I feel about Isaiah." He beckoned her toward a wooden bench, pulling out his handkerchief and dusting its surface to protect her clothing. "Come look at this passage."

Amelia sat on the rough-hewn bench, and Jared settled

next to her. She smelled so nice, a mixture of roses and spring flowers that made him want to breathe deeply.

He put the thought from his mind and opened his Bible and read the scripture aloud. Then he turned a few pages and read his favorite verse, Isaiah 40:31. " 'But they that wait upon the Lord shall renew their strength; they shall mount up with wings as eagles; they shall run, and not be weary; and they shall walk, and not faint.' "

"Those verses are certainly full of hope," Amelia conceded. "But what about all of the admonitions directed at the people of Israel? Didn't he spend a lot of time trying to warn them about following the path to destruction?"

Jared stared into Amelia's blue eyes. They reminded him of a clear mountain stream. He almost forgot what they were discussing as he gazed at her beautiful face. "Ummm. . . yes, you're right." He shook his head to clear it. "But Isaiah tempers his warnings with these words of hope. Words that can bring us peace in the midst of our darkest days."

"I never thought about it like that." She smiled at him.

Jared lost his train of thought once more. He closed his Bible and stood up. "I better get back inside. I'll be leaving soon. I'm going on to Knoxville."

"Me, too." She clapped her hands. "Maybe we'll see each other in Knoxville."

Was she flirting with him? What could such a lovely young woman see in a bookish fellow like him? Jared couldn't even figure out how to answer her. A large part of him wished it was likely that they'd run into each other again, but he doubted it. She would be attending parties and dances while he would spend all of his time studying.

Amelia stood and took his handkerchief from the bench. "Thank you for being so gallant."

He shook his head. "Keep it." He winced inwardly at the abrupt words. Why hadn't he paid more attention to the art of conversing with young women? He felt gauche and rude, but he didn't know how to soften his words. He was much better at writing than speaking. Finally, he settled on practicality. "It's probably time for breakfast."

After a brief silence, she let her hand fall to her side and moved to exit the garden. He followed her to the dining room, berating himself for not being more of a gentleman. He should have offered his arm to her. Why couldn't he be more self-assured? Why couldn't he find the right words for the occasion? Why did his tongue have to twist itself up into knots? Even if he did see Amelia after this trip, he was sure she would avoid him like the plague. And why shouldn't she?

Jared made quick work of his breakfast before seeking a seat on the ET&G, the train that would take him to Knoxville. Although he looked for Amelia and her traveling companions, he didn't see them again, even when the train stopped for lunch. He told himself it was for the best. Her guardian, Luke, would never allow him to speak to her. And even if he did, Jared still had no idea what to say to her.

four

Jared couldn't stop smiling. Two weeks at college, and everything was working out splendidly—well almost everything. He had a great roommate, Benjamin Montgomery, the youngest son of a local businessman. He and Benjamin had much in common, including older sisters and a love of the natural world. Of course, Benjamin was more interested in playing around than studying, but Jared was sure his attitude would change once they got into the full swing of the semester.

The only fly in Jared's ointment was a certain senior, Luke Talbot. He was the snobby fellow who'd escorted the beauteous Amelia on the train. And he'd made it clear that he had no time for underclassmen. But it would not be hard to avoid Mr. Talbot since they shared only chapel together. The seniors went to different classrooms, practiced their military exercises in a different area than the freshmen, and ate at different times.

With a shrug, Jared dismissed Luke Talbot from his thoughts and looked down at the flyer in his hand. It was an announcement for the first meeting of the Societas Philomathesian, a literary society at East Tennessee University. The door to his room opened, and Jared looked up to see Benjamin entering.

"I couldn't believe old Mr. Wallace surprised us with that test today." Benjamin tossed his book on their shared desk and threw himself across his bed.

"It wasn't so bad. He only asked questions from the chapter on regular Latin declensions."

Benjamin made a face at him. "He might as well have asked about cathedrals in France or shipping lanes in the Mediterranean."

A laugh bubbled up from Jared's chest. "Tell me you didn't say the same thing to Mr. Wallace."

A nod answered him. Benjamin Montgomery was a charmer who had won over most of their teachers within the first few days of his arrival. He was a good-looking man with a wiry strength that served him well on the parade grounds and large, deep blue eyes that held a hint of mischief all the time. He could say the most outrageous things, and the only response he got was appreciative laughter. Jared wished he had the same talent.

"You are incorrigible." Jared shook his head. "That would be a better line of questioning from Mr. Whitsell, our geography teacher."

"Geography, history, language, mathematics. All of it is nonsense. The only part of college that appeals to me is the military part." Benjamin sat on the edge of his bed and held his arms up, pretending to aim a rifle at the far wall. "I'm only attending ETU to please my parents. As soon as I finish here, I'm going to join up and shoot me some Yanks."

"What if I join the Yanks? Are you going to shoot me?"

Benjamin dropped his stance, and his mouth dropped open. His eyes, normally dark blue, turned almost purple in shock. "Fight with the Yanks? Now you sound like Whitsell, ready to betray your own countrymen."

"Don't tell me you haven't considered it. It's well known that Knoxville is divided. No matter which side you choose, you're likely to be fighting against someone you know."

A shrug was his only answer. "What are you reading?" asked Benjamin.

Jared held up the flyer in his hand. "The Societas Philomathesian is holding a meeting tomorrow night. Say you'll go with me." Jared knew it would be out of character for his roommate to attend something as serious as a literary society meeting, but he hoped to convince his friend. "I'll help you with your Latin verbs."

Benjamin stared at him for a full minute before answering. "I'll do it, but I want something more than a Latin tutor. I need a partner in crime."

"I don't know. . . . What kind of crime?"

"It won't be too bad. I just want to cause Mr. Wallace as much confusion as he caused me this morning."

Now it was Jared's turn to study his roommate's face as he considered his options. He could go alone to the society meeting and fade quietly into the background until he made new friends with similar interests, or he could yield to the temptation to do something daring. He'd never had much chance to be boyish at home, not with all those women around. And his pa was so starchy, he couldn't imagine Adam Stuart throwing caution to the wind. "I'll do it."

"It's a deal then." Benjamin stood up. "All we have to do is wait until everyone is asleep. I'll get the necessary equipment."

Jared took a deep breath and placed his hand in Benjamin's outstretched one. He hoped he would not regret his impulse.

❧

Jared pulled the slack out of the rope he and Benjamin had tied to the professors' doorknobs. All was quiet on the hall. The other students were snug in their beds, no doubt sleeping as he and his roommate should be doing. Instead, they had crept to the end of the floor where their professors slept in rooms directly across from each other. Following Benjamin's instructions, he had tied one end of their rope to Mr. Whitsell's doorknob. Benjamin looped the other end around Mr. Wallace's doorknob. He watched as his roommate tied a knot that would prevent either professor from opening his door in the morning.

"How long do you think it will take them to get free?"

Benjamin shushed him and returned his attention to their handiwork.

"What are you boys doing down there?" The whisper sounded as loud as a musket shot in the quiet hallway.

Jared gasped and jerked around to face the consequences of his actions. His whole life passed in front of his eyes in that brief moment. He would be sent home in disgrace. His parents would be so disappointed. Why had he ever agreed to such a silly prank?

His heart climbed up to his throat when a shaft of moonlight from a nearby window revealed Luke Talbot's wide shoulders and dark hair. He wished he could sink into the floorboards or disappear like a puff of smoke. Of all the people to catch them, why did it have to be a man who already despised him? "We're uh. . .we're—"

Benjamin pushed his way past Jared and stepped up to Luke. "We thought we heard a noise in the hall and came to investigate."

"Is that right?" Luke turned his attention on Benjamin. "And I suppose you have no idea who might have tied that rope to the professors' doorknobs?"

"I suppose it could have been any number of persons. Anyone with access to a length of rope who might also have a grudge against sneaky teachers who surprise unsuspecting freshmen with examinations."

"And what do you have to say to that?" Luke turned back to Jared.

He held out his hands, palms up, and shrugged. He was about to confess when Luke chuckled quietly. "Is Wallace still pulling those same old tricks? Maybe this will convince him to desist."

Jared could not have been more surprised if Luke had grown a tail and horns. This man had a sense of humor? He wasn't going to turn them in? They weren't going to be expelled?

"You two better get back to your room." Luke pointed a finger at them. "And don't think I'll be as lenient if I catch you out in the hallways after hours again."

Benjamin winked at Jared as they crept back to their room. Once they shut the door behind them, he slapped a hand on his chest and expelled a loud breath. "I thought we were done for when I heard him."

Jared undressed quickly and pulled on his nightshirt. "Me, too. I was already imagining the disgrace of being sent home before my first month had passed."

After they had both climbed into their beds, Jared lay still, contemplating the near disaster.

"I thought you said Luke Talbot was a pompous windbag." Benjamin's voice was thoughtful. "I have to disagree with your opinion. I think he's a regular sport."

Jared closed his eyes and sent a prayer of thankfulness to God that they had not been sent home in disgrace. "Yes, he was kind to let us go. But don't forget his warning." He turned over in the bed and punched his pillow. "I'm never going to give him or anyone else the chance to catch me again. From here on out, I'll be doing everything strictly by the rules."

❧

Jared could tell how much delight Benjamin was drawing from the commotion they'd caused, even though the two of them were not awake when the professors discovered they were trapped. By the time they dressed and headed for chapel, the row had died down, but the prank was the only topic being discussed. Who might have pulled such a trick? And done it without being caught?

"I hope they find out who did such an awful thing." Benjamin's blue eyes sparkled with mischief.

Jared winced, wishing his roommate was not quite so bold. "I'm glad no one was hurt."

"Don't be foolish. I heard they were set free within a matter of minutes. All it took was getting someone's attention."

The two of them entered the chapel, which buzzed like a hornet's nest. Everyone was whispering about the incident, shaking their heads and hiding smiles behind their hands.

Jared felt a little sick. He wished he'd never taken part. Perhaps if he went to the president and confessed his part, he would feel better. But what if he was expelled? And Benjamin, too? His head began to ache. He didn't know what to do.

A hand clamped down on his right shoulder, and Jared nearly yelped his surprise. He twisted quickly and looked into the frowning face of Luke Talbot. "You look a bit green about the gills, Stuart. Are you feeling sick?"

Jared shook his head but remained mute.

Luke leaned close and whispered into his ear. "If you're thinking about blabbing about what happened last night, you'd better think again. Any confession at this point would perforce include me, and I will not stand for that. I have a spotless record here, and no underclassman is going to ruin it. No harm was done. Go about your regular studies. By evening, this episode will be forgotten."

He nodded and slid into a pew. Mr. Wallace was leading the chapel service, and Jared was glad to see the man was his usual self, confident and a little pompous. His headache eased, his stomach settled down, and he concentrated on his prayer, thanking God for not getting caught and vowing to never again allow someone to drag him into another such incident.

The rest of the day passed without incident, for which Jared was thankful.

After dinner, he and Benjamin went to the Societas Philomathesian meeting, taking seats on the back row and listening as several members stood and read poetry, stories, or essays they'd written. His imagination was ignited. This is why he'd come to ETU—to be a part of such academic pursuits. He only wished he could think of a good subject to write about. His mind went to the Indians his parents worked so hard to protect, but that was their cause, not his. He listened to one fellow get up and read about the obligation of Southern men to join the Confederate Army, and Jared wondered why he was writing about his beliefs instead of fighting for them.

So caught up was Jared in the evening that he didn't realize how bored Benjamin was until he heard a soft buzzing sound. He looked over in horror to see his friend slumped down in the chair, his face dropped so far forward his chin rested on his chest. He elbowed Benjamin.

"Wha. . .what's the matter?"

"Shhh!" Jared put a finger across his lips in warning. "You fell asleep."

Benjamin frowned. "And you woke me? Is it time to go?"

Jared expelled a breath. "No."

"Okay then." Benjamin slouched once more and closed his eyes.

What had he expected? For Benjamin to suddenly gain an interest in literature? He sighed again. Benjamin raised one eyelid and peeked at him. He looked so innocent, so longsuffering. It was hard for Jared to hold on to his indignation. He could feel a grin teasing the corners of his mouth. How did Benjamin do it? He never seemed more than half serious about anything, but still he managed to charm his way through every circumstance. Jared wished some of that charm would rub off on him.

The meeting broke up, and he watched as Benjamin complimented each of the readers on his work, listening and nodding his head as one or another expounded further on his ideas. Jared chuckled to himself. If only they knew the truth.

"Did you enjoy the evening?" Benjamin asked as they made their way across campus to the dormitory.

"Very much. I want to write something and present it at the next meeting."

"Do you really?" Benjamin's voice was full of scorn. "I cannot imagine a duller group. But I guess it depends on your interests. My taste runs to more exciting pursuits, which puts me in mind of a favor I need to ask."

"Oh no." Jared opened the door of Southern Hall. The hallway was dimly lit as most students had already retired for the evening. "You're not going to get me involved in any more mischief."

"No," protested Benjamin. "It's nothing like that. Even I know when it's time to lie low. This has to do with my parents. Next week they're throwing a birthday party for a cousin of mine who recently came to town. She's from your part of the state—Nashville, or near to it. Anyway, my parents thought it would be nice to have a gathering of young people to help her feel more welcome."

"I don't know. Debutantes and parties are not my favorite pastimes. Besides, I have a lot of studying to do."

Benjamin's face took on the betrayed look of a heartbroken puppy. "You don't mean to make me go alone. I even told Ma I'd be bringing you with me."

"You told your mother without consulting me?" Jared shook his head. He really didn't want to go and didn't appreciate feeling manipulated. This was the perfect time to take a firm stand and refuse his roommate.

"We'll have a great time. We can skip the dinner and show up in time for the dancing." Benjamin bowed to an imaginary partner. "You'll have a great time. We'll make certain Cousin Amelia has sufficient dance partners to make her feel accepted, and then I promise to bring you straight back to your studies."

Jared's heart missed a beat and then compensated by doubling its speed. Amelia? Surely not the girl he'd seen on the train all those weeks ago? Was it possible? Knoxville was a large town, but how many young women had recently arrived there from Nashville? Curiosity and hope, a heady combination, filled his thoughts. How he would enjoy another opportunity to talk to her. He glanced at Benjamin and nodded. "I'll go."

"Great!" Benjamin slapped him on the back. "I knew I could count on you."

five

"Ouch." Amelia reached up and grabbed Tabitha's hand. "That's the third time you've pulled my hair. What's wrong?"

"Nothing. I'm sorry. I'll try to do better."

"Don't try that on me, Tabitha. I know you too well." She took the brush from Tabitha's hand and laid it on the dressing table, then turned to face her friend. "Tell me what's on your mind."

Tabitha's eyebrows drew together in a frown. "You need to go down soon. Turn around and let me finish your hair."

"Unh-unh." Amelia shook her head. "I'm not going down until I find out why you're acting so strangely."

"I. . .I can't talk about it." Tabitha turned away from her and faced the window.

Amelia said nothing. She and Tabitha had grown up together, even though Tabitha was a slave and she was the master's daughter. She had shared her dolls with Tabitha, and then when she learned to read, she'd shared her lessons with the young slave. Papa would skin both of them alive if he knew. It was illegal to teach a slave to read and write, but neither of them had considered the law when they were younger. As long as they never divulged the truth to anyone else, they would not get in trouble. Amelia's conscience pricked her a little at the thought. Was it wrong to lie to others for a good cause?

"It's. . .the c—cook's son." Tabitha's words were slow, as if she was carefully considering each one.

"The cook's son." Amelia clapped her hands together. "Is he handsome? Smart? Does he make your heart beat faster?"

"No, no." Tabitha turned to face her once again. "It's nothing like that. Nothing romantic. He...he's an escaped slave."

Amelia could feel a lump rise in her throat. She didn't like the sound of this, but she couldn't back out on her friend now. "Go on."

"He...he's a conductor."

The word fell between them like a boulder. A conductor. That meant he was part of the Underground Railroad. He was helping other slaves make their way to freedom. It was a noble cause, and one that Amelia would like to support, but she knew better. Hadn't she already paid a high enough price for her dealings with slaves? She looked at Tabitha's troubled face. "I see."

"He's got a group out in the barn. One of them's been shot. A young boy."

The blood drained from Amelia's face as she considered the pain and fear the child must be feeling. "What happened?"

Tabitha knelt on the floor in front of her. Tears ran down her cheeks. "You know there's safe places where runaways can hide out."

Amelia nodded. No one knew exactly how many slaves had found their way to freedom in the past decade. Or how many had died trying. People caught harboring runaway slaves were breaking the law. It was a scary choice to make, especially since Tennessee had seceded from the Union last spring.

In the short time she'd been here, Amelia had discovered Knoxville was a town divided over the issue of abolition. Some believed each state should have the right to decide whether or not to outlaw slavery, while others were staunchly opposed to allowing slavery at all, and still others depended on slave labor to run profitable businesses. Even though she had found her aunt and uncle to be a little more liberal in their attitude toward slavery, she would never have dreamed of this possibility. "Are you saying my aunt and uncle are helping slaves get free?"

"Oh my, no." Tabitha placed her hands over Amelia's. "They'd have a fit for sure. But it's the cook's son. He's in a bad fix. The station where he was supposed to hide was found out, and the escapees were almost captured. So he brought them here and asked his ma to help."

A knock on the door made both girls jump.

"Stand up," Amelia whispered. Then more loudly she called out, "Who's there?"

"Amelia, honey, it's about time for you to come downstairs." Aunt Laura's voice was bright and cheerful. She was obviously looking forward to the party, having no idea that disaster could strike the whole family at any moment.

"I'll be right down," Amelia tried for a light tone to match her aunt's. "Tabitha is putting the final touches on my coiffure."

"All right, dear. Your uncle and I will be waiting for you."

Amelia held her breath until she heard her aunt's receding footsteps. She turned to Tabitha. "I can finish my hair. You go and help the cook's son. I won't need you any more tonight."

A slight smile turned up the corners of Tabitha's mouth. "You'd look a sight for sure. You don't know anything about fixing hair."

The clock on her mantel ticked away the minutes as Tabitha expertly twisted her hair up off Amelia's neck and fastened it into place with jeweled pins. A few tendrils escaped on either side of her face and at the nape of her neck, giving her a soft but sophisticated look.

"You look real nice. You're going to be the prettiest girl

at the party." Tabitha's words did not match her expression, which was still drawn in a frown.

"Thank you, Tabitha." A few days ago Amelia had been so excited about her new gown. It was one of her fanciest, a daring style that bared her arms and nipped in at her waist before expanding outward to form a wide bell that swayed as she moved. Now she was more concerned with the dire straits of the people hidden out back.

She stood and went to her bureau, thankful she had thought to bring her medicine bag, and pulled out strips of bandaging and forceps. "I don't know exactly what you may need, but this should help."

"Thank you." Tabitha tucked the forceps into the belt at her waist and dropped the bandaging into her pocket. Then she walked to Amelia's bed and picked up the Spanish lace shawl she'd laid across it earlier. "You need this." She arranged the soft material over Amelia's arms to fall just below her shoulders, then pushed her toward the door. "Go enjoy your party and don't worry none."

"Please be careful." Concern made Amelia's throat tighten. She would rather have helped Tabitha than go downstairs and play the part of an empty-headed debutante. "Promise you'll come get me if you need help."

Tabitha nodded and shooed her out of the room.

Lord, please protect my friend and those poor souls she's trying to help. Her prayer brought Amelia a feeling of peace as she descended her aunt and uncle's narrow staircase, but she wished she could do more.

She took a deep breath and concentrated on the designs on Aunt Laura's flocked velvet wallpaper. It was a new pattern, forest green in color with small birds perched on wide oak leaves. Aunt Laura had glowed with pleasure when Amelia had complimented it.

Amelia's skirts brushed both the polished balustrade and the wallpaper as she descended. Her heart was pumping hard by the time she reached the first-floor landing, and she pinned a wide smile on her face. She pushed her worries about the slaves to the back of her mind. It was very thoughtful of her relatives to have planned this party for her, and she was determined to enjoy it. . .or at least appear to.

Her aunt and uncle were a sweet couple, both somewhat rounded from their comfortable lifestyle. Uncle Francis, a canny investor with an eye to the future, had made a fortune by purchasing stock in such inventions as a machine for drilling through rocks, boilers for use with the new steam engines, and Elisha Otis's hoisting apparatus that moved cargo vertically. Uncle Francis had explained to her the uses for such a contraption, but Amelia could not understand his enthusiasm. Whatever its purpose, the device had earned her uncle an ample income, enough so he could spend most of his days enjoying the company of his peers at a gentlemen's club downtown.

Aunt Laura was a collector. She loved filling her home with fancy furniture and stylish knickknacks. Nearly every surface held some interesting object that her aunt loved to talk about. She was like one of the birds on her wallpaper, collecting leaves, twigs, and bits of fluff for her nest. Together, her aunt and uncle made a charming couple, quite different from what she expected when Papa banished her. She had thought she'd find herself in a prison-like atmosphere, surrounded by sour jailors who resented her presence. How wrong she had been.

"There she is." Uncle Francis's booming voice was as warm as a summer breeze. He chucked her under the chin. "You're as pretty as a picture, m'dear."

"Thank you, Uncle." Even though Amelia only stood some

three inches above five feet, she was as tall as he, although his girth easily outstripped hers. Dark blue eyes, a Montgomery family trait, twinkled at her above his beard and mustache. He was dressed in a brown cutaway coat with a gold vest underneath, his attire showing that he kept abreast of current fashion. "You're looking quite handsome yourself."

She turned to her aunt, who was resplendent in a gown of rich puce satin. Tiny pearl buttons decorated the bodice from the collar to her waist. The sleeves were wide at the shoulder and elbow and tapered to a narrow cuff fastened with more pearl buttons. The skirt, made of the same material as the bodice, was full and boasted a deep flounce. "And you are also looking lovely this evening, Aunt Laura."

"What a sweet child." Aunt Laura wrapped her in a perfumed embrace. "Always saying the nicest things to your old aunt and uncle."

Amelia emerged laughing. "It's easy when I am staying with such kind, handsome hosts. How many guests do you expect to have this evening?"

"Only a small, intimate group for dinner," her aunt answered. "Our son, Benjamin, will be here, along with some new friends of his from college. And a few friends of mine from around town will be coming, with their sons and daughters."

Uncle Francis cleared his throat. "Our dinner table will only accommodate forty guests, so we were quite limited in our selection. But never fear, many more will join us after dinner for the ball."

Aunt Laura nodded. "I wouldn't be surprised if we had upwards of two hundred guests."

"I see." Amelia tried to keep the trepidation from her voice. Forty guests for dinner? And many more later? She hoped she could find enough unexceptional subjects to discuss. Growing up on a remote, self-sustaining plantation had not prepared her for fancy parties or witty dinner conversation. She prayed she would not embarrass her hosts by saying or doing something to mark herself as provincial.

She prayed even more for Tabitha, as she knew what occupied her mind most were those attempting to gain their freedom. . .and her inability to tamp her desire to help.

❧

It was easy to see which house belonged to Benjamin's parents from the number of carriages lined up in front, waiting to disgorge their passengers onto the brightly lit stoop. An unexpected feeling of homesickness swept over Jared as he was reminded of parties his own parents and great-aunt had hosted for one or the other of his sisters.

A slave hurried to take their horses. He slid from the saddle, ready to be free of the tired mount he'd rented from a livery stable near the college. His horse had been only slightly faster than walking across town. Benjamin's sleek roan, a stallion he'd raised from a colt, had fought his rider all the way, trying to move at a gait faster than amble.

Jared brushed his coat and straightened his cravat. "I was beginning to think we wouldn't arrive until after the party was over." When he received no response, he looked up to see that Benjamin was halfway up the front steps. With a sigh, he hurried after his friend.

At the front door, he had a moment to take in the scene before being introduced to Mr. and Mrs. Montgomery. He could see no sign of the cousin who was the guest of honor. His gaze lit on a tall, thin girl with curly brown hair who was standing slightly behind Benjamin's mother. That must be her. His dreams of renewing his acquaintance with the girl on the train died a quick death. He could feel his smile slipping, but his sympathy was roused by the obvious discomfort on the young lady's face. He shook hands with Benjamin's parents when introduced then turned to the poor uncomfortable girl.

"This must be the sweet cousin I've heard so much about." He smiled down at her, hoping to ease her discomfort. "Hello, I'm Jared Stuart, Benjamin's roommate at East Tennessee University."

The young lady's mouth dropped open in shock. He wondered at her surprise. She was the guest of honor, after all. She dropped a stiff curtsy as he bowed.

She said nothing, so he cast about in his mind for something to say. "I understand that you are also from Nashville, where my family now resides."

"N–no, sir." Her voice was so low he had to bend forward to make out what she was saying. "I. . .my. . .fa–family is fr–from Knoxville."

Jared frowned. Had he been mistaken? He looked around for Benjamin and spotted his friend some distance away, standing on the edge of a circle of guests. He turned back to the girl, who looked like she'd rather be anywhere than standing next to him. Her hands picked at the material of her skirt, and her gaze flitted from one place to another in the room.

"There you are, Faye." A round-faced woman in a white dress more suited to a debutante than a matron advanced on them. Her brown hair was pulled tightly back from her face and disappeared under a fancy lace kerchief. She turned a smile on Jared, making him feel a little like a rabbit about to become dinner for a mountain lion. "And who is your new friend?"

The girl swallowed twice and shook her head.

Irritation was evident on her mother's face, but she pushed it back and smiled at him. "Hello, I am Beatrice Downing. I see you've already met my daughter."

So this was not Benjamin's cousin. Jared introduced himself again and made his escape as quickly as possible without appearing rude. As the orchestra began tuning up in preparation for the dancing, he strolled over to the knot of people to find Benjamin. Why had his roommate deserted him amongst all these strangers?

The thought was swept away when he saw the person Benjamin was talking to. It was Amelia, his Amelia, the girl who'd captured his imagination and appeared in his dreams with regularity. The girl who'd intrigued him from the first moment he saw her. She was standing at the very center of the group, which he now realized consisted only of young men. These men were acting like idiots, vying for her attention, offering her outrageous compliments, and begging her to dance with them.

Benjamin elbowed his way past a few of them. "I'm afraid I must claim precedence." He bowed over her hand. "It's nice to see you again, Cousin Amelia."

Several of her admirers groaned, and one of them complained loudly that Benjamin was not giving the rest of them a sporting chance.

Her laughing blue eyes made Jared catch his breath. She was adorable. It was no wonder all the young men crowded around her. Even now, he could see a blush of innocence cresting her cheeks. She turned to the young man who had complained. "I am sorry, sir." Her voice held a note of sincerity. "You and your friends have been very kind, but I must give precedence to my family."

"May I call on you tomorrow morning?" The young man's disappointment of a moment ago seemed to have disappeared. "I have a nice carriage. Perhaps I can take you for a ride in the park."

"I appreciate your kindness, Mr. Castlewhite, but I already have another commitment."

A chorus of groans came from the others standing near her, but before they could begin to importune the young lady, Benjamin put her hand on his arm and pulled her away.

"I have a very special friend I'd like you to meet, cousin." He pulled her toward Jared. "Jared Stuart, please meet my cousin, Amelia Montgomery."

"It's you." Her eyes, so deep, so mysterious, shone in the light of the candles. "I never got to say good-bye."

"You two know each other?" Benjamin's shocked gaze met Jared's sheepish one. "Have you been keeping secrets from me?"

"We rode the train together, but we were never properly introduced." Jared raised his spectacles to the bridge of his nose. "Luke Talbot made sure of that."

Benjamin's laughter turned heads in the room. "So that is the reason for—"

"Did you finish *A Tale of Two Cities*?" Jared interrupted Benjamin.

"Yes. I found it very thought provoking."

"Oh no. Spare me." Benjamin looked from one to the other. He rolled his eyes. "Please tell me you are not as bookish as Jared."

"I hesitate to disappoint you, cousin." She answered Benjamin's question, but Jared could feel her gaze on him. "I must confess that Mr. Stuart and I share a love of Charles Dickens."

Jared felt as invincible as a conqueror. "If you're not going to dance with Miss Montgomery, perhaps you will allow me to?"

Amelia glanced at her cousin, a question in her gaze. Benjamin's lips curled slightly. "It doesn't look like I have much choice." He bowed and left them standing on the edge of the ballroom floor.

Jared was finally thankful for the dancing lessons his parents had insisted on. He could partner Miss Montgomery without fear of appearing gauche. He placed one hand at her waist and held out the other for her to grasp before sweeping her into the midst of the other dancers. The feeling of holding her close was heady, but it also caused him to lose the ability to converse. He could feel tension tightening his shoulders as he searched his empty mind for something to say to her. Should he compliment her gracefulness on the dance floor? Or her pretty dress?

"Have you found time to read Mr. Dickens's book, Mr. Stuart?"

"Yes, it was one of my first purchases when I reached Knoxville." Jared felt his tension easing. He could discuss books all day long. "Tell me, were you as horrified as I by the marquis' brutal treatment of those in his power?"

"Yes." Amelia shuddered. "I was not at all disappointed by his demise."

They spent the rest of the waltz discussing the themes of sacrifice and justice explored by Charles Dickens in his novels. So lost was he in their discussion that Jared was surprised when the orchestra stopped playing. He escorted her from the floor, reluctant to give her over to one of her other admirers.

"Good evening, Miss Montgomery."

The deep voice brought Jared's head up. He nearly groaned as he recognized Luke Talbot. He should have known the man would be here.

Talbot's dark eyes were fixed on Amelia. Jared doubted the man had even noticed him. "It's such a pleasure to see you tonight, Amelia."

"Hello, Luke. I'm glad you were able to come." She took her hand from Jared's arm and held it out to Talbot. "You remember Mr. Stuart, whom we met on the train."

"Ah, if it's not the midnight wanderer." Luke's voice was full of mockery. "Where is your nefarious partner?"

Jared could feel heat rising to his cheeks. His ears grew so hot he thought steam might be rising from them. "Mr. Talbot."

Amelia's brow wrinkled. "Must you talk in riddles, Luke?"

"I'm referring to a small matter that occurred at the college last week." Luke's confident smile was turned to Amelia. "It's nothing to concern your pretty head about."

Somehow, Luke had managed to once again place himself between Jared and Amelia. Jared watched helplessly as the self-assured man skillfully drew her away from those who were vying for her attention and led her to a corner of the ballroom next to a large plant.

The next hour passed slowly. Jared partnered several young women, but they all seemed shallow and grasping in contrast to Amelia. He was relieved when Mr. Montgomery sent the orchestra on a break and announced it was time for his niece to receive her special birthday gift.

It took two servants to bring in the tall, sheet-draped gift. They put their burden on the floor at Amelia's feet.

She tugged the covering off to reveal a gilded birdcage hung from an ornate stand. A small tree had been wound around the bars of the cage on one side, its branches providing a perch for the small, black-tailed, gray bird inside.

"It's a mockingbird," explained Amelia's aunt. "We thought you would enjoy hearing its songs. It is quite the mimic, you know, and should fill your room with the most delightful sounds."

Jared watched Amelia's expression as she cooed to the frightened bird. Did she feel as sad as he did to see the poor thing trapped in a cage? She seemed satisfied with the gift. But maybe she was only being polite. He knew politeness was bred in young ladies from an early age. Amelia would never be ungracious about a gift.

Yes, he nodded to himself. That must be the explanation. A wonderful idea came to him. He would come to visit her tomorrow and offer to set the poor bird free for her. Together they could come up with an acceptable excuse to appease her aunt and uncle. He would ask her tonight about visiting and perhaps even hint at his plan. He would have to be careful, but Jared felt he could summon the requisite amount of delicacy and depend on Amelia's astuteness to grasp his intent.

six

Amelia laughed, but the sound seemed brittle to her ears. The brightest spot in her evening had been meeting Jared Stuart once again. He was such a fascinating young man. She would like to know him better and wondered if he would come by to visit. Probably not. University students did not have much free time.

But even meeting the interesting Mr. Stuart could not completely turn her mind from the drama occurring in her relatives' stable. She was worried about Tabitha and wondered if she could escape the party for a few minutes to check on her. But the orchestra was still playing, and she still had to dance with one callow boy after another.

Her current partner, Reginald something or other, reeked of pomade and citrus cologne. He had the beginnings of a mustache that unfortunately emphasized his overlong nose and did nothing to hide a mouthful of crooked teeth. He had asked her about the weather and was currently going into great detail about winter and his hopes for an early spring planting.

She wanted to pull away from the poor fellow and escape, especially when she saw Luke Talbot taking his leave of her aunt and uncle. She would have liked to spend more time with him and find out what he'd meant by calling Jared Stuart a midnight wanderer. But it looked as if even that would be denied her. As Reginald pulled her around the floor, she saw Luke's tall form exiting the ballroom. Finally, the dance came to an end, and she escaped her partner.

Aunt Laura was showing off Amelia's birthday gift to a couple of matrons while Uncle Francis bid good night to an older couple. A red-haired young man bearing down on her position at the edge of the dance floor had Amelia turning away quickly. She pretended to trip and faked a groan. She told the approaching suitor she had to repair her dress and hurried to the nearest exit, proud of her quick thinking.

The narrow hall leading to the back door was cool and quiet. The crisp air felt good for a few minutes in contrast to the overheated ballroom, but as she reached to open the door, Amelia wished she'd brought her shawl with her. It was lying across the back of a chair in the ballroom, so she would have to do without it.

The back door opened and Amelia caught her breath, releasing it all at once when she recognized Tabitha's high cheekbones and simple hairstyle.

"What are you doing here?" Tabitha glanced over her shoulder before stepping into the hallway and closing the door. "You need to get back to your birthday party. Someone will come looking for you."

"I thought you might need help. How are they?"

"Scared, as you can imagine. But safe for the moment." Tabitha looked down at her apron, and Amelia realized it was streaked with dirt and blood.

"Are you hurt?" Amelia looked for signs of a wound.

Tabitha shook her head. "I had to bandage the child."

"Was there a bullet? Did you get it out?" Amelia fired the questions out in quick succession. "Was anyone else hurt?"

Tabitha's smile showed her weariness. "Yes, no, and no."

"You didn't remove the bullet?"

"It went straight through the little boy's arm." She sighed. "It broke a bone on the way."

Amelia winced.

"I've seen worse back home during the harvest." Tabitha's voice sounded weary.

Amelia knew it was true. Accidents and sickness occurred, even on a plantation that was as progressively run as Papa's. She and Mama had spent many an afternoon patching up machete injuries and setting broken bones. But they'd never had to deal with a bullet wound. Mama had showed her how to treat such wounds this summer after Tennessee seceded from the Union. Who knew when the need to treat bullet wounds might arise? Mama believed it was their duty to be prepared for such an eventuality.

"Infection is the biggest danger then." Amelia took Tabitha's hand in her own and squeezed. "I know you did a good job, but I'd like to see the child for myself."

The back door opened again, and the cook and some of the staff filed in one by one. Amelia registered their surprise and fear at her presence.

Tabitha took a few minutes to reassure them before leading Amelia to the stable out back.

The wooden structure was dark and quiet since Uncle Francis had hired a public livery stable down the street for the guests' horses. Amelia stood still for a moment, waiting for her eyes to adapt to the darkness. The night air seemed to absorb sounds and made Amelia feel miles away from the music and dancing of the birthday ball.

Tabitha pursed her lips and whistled, moving her mouth and tongue so that the sound imitated the call of a bird. Another bird warbled some feet ahead of where they stood.

"It's Tabitha. I have a friend with me."

The darkness near the stable door seemed to thicken and became a short, stocky man whom Amelia recognized as the Montgomerys' senior coachman. He waved them inside the stable. Not a word was spoken as he led them to the rear of the building and opened the door of the room used to store saddles and bridles. A kerosene lantern flickered in the corner of the tiny room, highlighting the frightened, dark faces of half-a-dozen occupants.

A muscular man pushed himself from the floor and stood to face Amelia and Tabitha. "What are you doing here?"

His smooth, dark skin stretched across high cheekbones, and intelligence shone from his coffee-brown eyes. His dark clothing looked tattered, but he held himself with all the self-assurance of a prince—chin up, shoulders straight, and legs wide. He crossed his arms across his broad chest and stared at her.

Tabitha bit her lip and looked toward Amelia. "This is Melek, Cook's son. Melek, this is Amelia. She's a friend who knows medicine. She's come to look at Nebo's arm."

"You trust her?" Melek's voice was deep and full of suspicion.

Amelia understood his doubt. Someone who accepted strangers easily would soon be caught by bounty hunters and sold back into slavery or hung for treason. She stepped forward. "I would never betray you or those you are trying to help." She lifted her chin and refused to back down as Melek glared at her. Her heart thumped so hard she thought the people in the room might be able to hear it. What was she doing here? She could be inside dancing the night away instead of standing in a dark barn confronting an angry man. Yet something compelled her to her present actions.

No one spoke for a moment, and the tension built. But

then one small sound changed everything. A quiet moan.

Amelia remembered why she had come. She followed the sound to a mound of what she'd taken to be rags. This must be the child.

"Nebo." She whispered the word and was rewarded when a dark head raised up from the ragged coverings.

The other people in the room faded as she knelt next to the young boy and checked his arm, then placed a hand on his hot forehead. "You're a very brave boy."

Amelia pushed herself up from the floor and faced the cook's son. "I have some willow bark in my room. I can send it down to your mother to make a tea for the child. It should bring him some ease and may reduce his fever."

He inclined his head slightly. "Thank you."

She nodded to the others in the room. "Do you need anything else?"

"Only that you will not speak of our presence here."

She straightened her shoulders and stared directly into his eyes. "I would never do such a thing."

"I hope your words are true, not the changing songs of the mockingbird."

A laugh broke out as she thought of the gift she had received for her birthday. "Your secret is safe with me."

❧

A blush heated Amelia's cheeks as she hurried down the hall to a mirror to check her appearance before returning to the ballroom. She groaned at the bedraggled woman who stared back at her.

Tabitha had fixed rosebuds in her hair earlier this evening, but they had slipped toward her right ear. She poked and prodded at the silly things until they once again perched across the center part in her hair. Pulling a pin from another part of her head, she affixed the flowers and nodded briefly. She opened her fan and waved it in front of her hot cheeks. It wouldn't do to return to the guests flushed.

Amelia glanced downward and groaned. Her skirt was a mess. She smoothed it as much as possible without help and picked off a couple of strands of straw that had clung to the material when she knelt to care for poor little Nebo. Amelia would have liked to escape upstairs, change clothes, and go back to the stable to watch over the child. But that option was out of the question. She squared her shoulders and practiced a smile before turning from the mirror.

The orchestra was taking a break, so the people in the ballroom were standing in small groups talking as she made her entrance. She glanced around to find Jared, eager to resume their conversation about Mr. Dickens and his novels.

"Where have you been, cousin?" Benjamin's deep voice tickled her ear.

Amelia jumped slightly. She'd not realized anyone was behind her. She spun around and opened her fan, waving it briskly in front of her face. "I had a slight tear in my flounce." The lie slipped easily between her lips and guilt made her heart beat faster. She hadn't had much practice at telling untruths. "It took me awhile to get it mended."

Benjamin nodded. He spread a hand to indicate the ballroom. "It seems your ardent swains have given up, and I must say I'm relieved. This is the first time I've gotten to talk to you without being elbowed by a dozen eager suitors."

"Your mother and father have been very kind to introduce me to their friends." Amelia glanced around the room, hoping to find Jared Stuart, but she could not spot his slender figure. "I'm sure everyone was being kind to me because I'm a newcomer."

Her cousin raised an eyebrow and started talking about her taking the town by storm, but Amelia didn't pay him much attention. She wasn't interested in making a splash in Knoxville society.

Where had Jared gone? Had he left for the evening? Disappointment pulled her lips down, but then she straightened her spine. She would not allow the absence of one guest to disturb her. She had more important things to worry about. Like how little Nebo was doing. Amelia could hardly wait for the party to end so she could return to check on the child.

Momentary regret for her involvement with the Underground Railroad was pushed to the back of her mind. What choice did she have? She would never be able to live with herself if she didn't do what she could to make the slaves' flight successful.

Even as she smiled at her cousin and pretended to be flattered by his compliments, part of her mind made a list of necessities to smuggle to the hidden refugees.

seven

As he walked across the campus, Jared pulled up the collar of his greatcoat. The rough wool scratched his chin, but the material kept cold air from reaching his neck. He waved at one of the freshmen as they passed each other but did not stop to talk. It was far too brisk out this morning, and he wanted to get to class in plenty of time to hear the lecture. He lowered his head and trudged onward through the cool, morning air.

"Wait up." Benjamin's deep voice drew his attention from the frosty ground.

Jared looked over his shoulder and let out an exasperated sigh. "I thought you were going to march with the early parade and go to Whitsell's makeup class since you performed so poorly on that last geography exam."

A shrug answered him. Benjamin's mischievous grin appeared, raising Jared's suspicions. "Maybe I wanted to hear the infamous newspaper editor."

"I wish William Brownlow had been able to come." Jared turned back to the pathway leading to North College, the name given to the northernmost building of the university.

Benjamin caught up with him and slung an arm over his shoulder. "I know. But after all the strife he was igniting with the anti-secession views in his newspaper, it's no wonder he had to run for his life. If the people of East Tennessee had gotten their way, you and I would be Unionists instead of Johnny Rebs. Since the occupation of the Confederate Army, things have been tense between the two groups, and his inflammatory pieces weren't helping much."

"Inflammatory pieces?" Jared shook off his friend's arm. "Didn't he have the right to print what he believed?"

"Don't get angry with me." Benjamin raised both his hands as if he was preparing to ward off a blow. "I didn't say there wasn't some truth in his articles, but you read them. In fact you read several of them to me. You have to admit Parson Brownlow doesn't know the meaning of tact."

"It's not a newspaper's job to be tactful. Every newspaper has a duty to inform its readers of the facts. Don't you remember studying Thomas Carlyle's reference to reporters as the Fourth Estate? He believed it was more important than the church, the nobility, or the middle class. Although I disagree with his putting journalists above the importance of the church, I do believe they hold great power and even greater responsibility, especially now that we are at war." Jared realized he'd stopped walking. He was going to be late. And he'd wanted to be early. "I don't want to debate this with you, Benjamin. I'm going to class. I'm sure Martin Stone has a lot to say about the importance of newspaper publishing. He is the editor of the *Tennessee Tribune*, and it's become the largest publication since Brownlow's *Whig* was put out of business." He started walking again.

"You're right." Benjamin matched his pace. "Why do you think I decided to tag along this morning?"

Jared didn't answer. He reached the steps of North College and bounded up them two at a time. He pulled open the heavy door and held it open for Benjamin to precede him. "I don't really know why you're here. You've never shown the least interest in writing."

Benjamin pushed his chest out. "I'm turning over a new

leaf. I'm going to concentrate on writing." He linked his arm through Jared's as they climbed the stairs to the second floor. "Maybe we can open a newspaper of our own. Isn't that how your hero Brownlow got started? Then we can publish our own beliefs and change the world."

A snort escaped Jared. "Don't you remember how you struggled over that essay last week? I doubt you are eager to become a writer."

"Maybe you could do the writing." Benjamin grinned at him. "And I can manage the other aspects of the business. Think of how famous we'll be when *our* efforts end the war."

Benjamin's words seemed to echo in the wide hallway. Jared was reminded of his belief that words really could make a difference. Excitement buzzed through him. "The pen is mightier than the sword, right?"

"I don't know about all that," Benjamin answered. "But it's certainly much lighter to wield."

❧

Amelia sneaked down to the barn before joining her aunt and uncle at the breakfast table. Little Nebo's forehead was hot, but that was to be expected. She coaxed him to drink another draught of the willow bark tea Melek's mother, the cook, had prepared. When she pulled away the bandage covering his arm, she was relieved to see it was not swollen or draining. She glanced at Melek, who watched her from one corner of the tack room.

Melek asked, "What is your opinion, little mockingbird?"

"I think he will recover."

"Can he travel today?"

She shook her head as she replaced the dressing. "He needs sleep to fully recover."

"If he is caught here, his captors will not be concerned about his rest."

Amelia's lips straightened. "Would you rather kill him yourself by moving him too soon?"

Silence was her only answer. She finished her work and looked around. At least six people crowded in the little room. "Does anyone else need my help?"

Declining whispers and headshakes answered her. Amelia pushed herself up from the pallet holding Nebo and closed her bag of medicines.

Melek escorted her from the room. "Thank you."

"I will check back later."

"No. You must stay away or your family may become suspicious."

His warning echoed in her mind as Amelia hurried to the breakfast room. She seated herself and bowed her head briefly over the plate that was set in front of her. When she had finished blessing her food, she listened to her uncle's latest diatribe.

"I'm afraid women simply don't understand these things." Uncle Francis's comment was not intended to irritate Amelia, but that's the effect it had. Her mouth dropped open, but he continued on, oblivious to her consternation. "Tennessee had no choice but to secede from the Union when Lincoln called for troops to fight against our brothers at Fort Sumter."

A thousand emotional retorts filled her imagination, but Amelia opted for logic. "Then why did Kentucky refuse to follow our lead?"

Uncle Francis shook his head and glanced toward Aunt Laura before answering Amelia's question. "My dear, suffice it to say Kentucky has many reasons to declare neutrality. Politics are often convoluted. Better to ask whether our brothers in Kentucky wish to abolish slavery. The answer would be a resounding no." He folded the newspaper he'd been reading and slapped it against the table for emphasis. "I have little doubt Kentucky will bow to the inevitable before the end of the year and join the Confederacy."

"I'm sure you're right, my dear." Aunt Laura washed a bite of toast down with her cup of tea. "If the war lasts that long. I pray every night it will end before any more young men are killed or wounded. I'm so concerned about our son's eagerness to join the fighting."

"I don't want to see him enlist any more than you do, but Benjamin is a grown man. We raised him to take pride in his heritage." Uncle Francis reached a hand across the table, palm up. "We must allow him to make his own decisions even if we'd prefer to keep him safe at home."

Aunt Laura placed her hand in his. The look that passed between them was full of love and tenderness.

A rush of empathy filled Amelia. Her aunt and uncle were good people. They were obviously worried about their son's future. And hadn't they welcomed her with open arms? They'd made sure she was introduced to all the right people. She appreciated the lavish ball they'd thrown for her birthday and felt more than a little guilt over helping the escaping slaves when she knew her relatives would never approve of her actions.

Aunt Laura pulled her hand away and turned her gaze to Amelia. Her eyes were suspiciously bright, but she cleared her throat and forced her lips into a shaky smile. "What do you have planned for today, my dear?"

Amelia was thankful for the change of subject. "Luke Talbot is supposed to come over later this morning. We are going riding in the park."

"That Talbot fellow is getting to be a regular visitor." Uncle Francis raised his eyebrows. "I don't know when he has time for studies."

A blush crept up Amelia's throat and heated her face. "Luke has always been like an older brother to me."

"Yes, I thought at first that was his reason for coming over, to make sure you were comfortable in your new surroundings." Aunt Laura's smile widened. "But you have been with us for almost two months now. He must have some other compelling reason to continue his attentions."

"Why would he not?" Uncle Francis winked at his wife. "Our niece is as pretty as a picture and sweet natured to boot. Half the young men in Knoxville are trying to turn her head."

Amelia pressed a hand against her hot cheek. "You're the one turning my head, Uncle. I'm sure the only reason they are interested is because I am a novelty."

"Has your new riding habit arrived, dear?"

"Yes, ma'am. It's lovely." Amelia poured her enthusiasm for the new ensemble into her voice. "I can hardly wait to wear it." She thought of the short braided jacket and white garibaldi shirt that lent the riding outfit a militaristic appearance. The skirt was long and full to allow her freedom, whether she was seated on a horse or walking.

"I'm sure you'll cut quite the figure." Uncle Francis's voice was warm to match his smile. "The other young ladies had better look to their swains, or they are likely to lose them."

Amelia pushed back her chair and ran to hug her uncle. "You are undoubtedly prejudiced, but I appreciate your kind words."

"Go on, child." He laughed and shooed her out of the room.

Her conscience, which had been temporarily silenced by the affection of her aunt and uncle, roared once again as she saw the front page of the paper lying on the table. It was full of advertisements seeking information on runaway slaves and promising huge rewards for their return. As she trudged upstairs, Amelia wondered how she would ever reconcile her world with her morals and her faith.

Tabitha was waiting for her in the bedroom and helped Amelia don her new riding habit. Her admiring gaze met Amelia's in the mirror. "You do look a sight."

A heavy sigh filled Amelia's chest and escaped her in a rush. She was the most hypocritical creature on the planet. Here she was concentrating on new clothes when there was so much she ought to be doing instead.

"Whatever is the matter with you today?"

Amelia turned and faced Tabitha. "How can you stay here with me?"

"I. . .I don't know what you mean."

"Don't be ridiculous, Tabitha. I know you too well. You're smart and pretty. You must have thought about running away."

Tabitha turned away and busied herself with folding Amelia's nightgown and wrapper before storing them in the cedar chiffonier next to her dressing table.

"Don't you want to leave this household and taste freedom for yourself? Don't you want to use the Underground Railroad? Meet someone special? Start a family and know that your children and your children's children will grow up safe and able to determine their own futures?"

Tabitha turned to look at her, a frown marring her wide brow. "Of course I've thought of it." She paused as if considering her words. "Not everyone is as brave as you."

"Brave?" Now it was Amelia's turn to frown. "I'm not brave at all. In fact, I have been wondering all morning why I do nothing to fight against a system that I abhor."

"It was brave of you to risk your reputation to help Melek and the others last night."

"Yes, I risked my reputation. But that's nothing compared to you and the others. You risked your very lives. If I had been caught, my aunt and uncle would have been scandalized—they might have even returned me to my parents. I can understand Cook helping her son. But you and the other slaves will most likely be hung for your involvement if you're discovered aiding Melek."

"We all risk a great deal." Tabitha walked to the birdcage and pulled off its cover. Amelia's mockingbird hopped onto its perch and opened its beak. A song as bright as the sun outside filled the bedroom. "But it was worth the risk to know they will soon live free."

Amelia's breath caught. "That's what I mean. Don't you want to go with them? Don't you want to experience freedom and not live in fear?"

Tabitha giggled. "I don't fear you. Aren't we friends? Didn't you teach me to read? I am content to stay where I am for now."

"I wish I could find my own way to contentment."

Tabitha laughed.

"What?" asked Amelia, hurt that her friend was making light of something that bothered her so.

"I don't know. It seems funny to me that you have so much and yet complain that you are not content." She stopped and looked at Amelia. "We are both blessed. We live in a beautiful house, we have full bellies, and we're surrounded by friends."

"Yes. I know I should be counting my blessings. And yet how can I when I am part of a culture that treats human beings as property?" She pointed to the wide four-poster piled high with feather mattresses and quilts. "Slaves have no more right to demand consideration than that bed over there."

Tabitha's eyes narrowed. " 'Who knoweth whether thou art come to the kingdom for such a time as this?' "

The biblical quote shocked Amelia into silence. Was God planning to use her as He had used Esther? Could she be instrumental in the deliverance of slaves? Hope blossomed in her chest like an early spring. A little voice, her conscience perhaps, whispered that she could not be chosen. People who were chosen were not so riddled with doubt. "I don't have the ear of President Jefferson Davis. I can do very little."

"You may be right." Tabitha looked toward the mocking-bird, who was singing through his litany of calls. He whistled, tweeted, squawked, and chirped, mocking the songs of birds from the Acadian flycatcher to the whip-poor-will. "But God can do anything. And He will, whether it is through your efforts or through someone else's."

Amelia pondered Tabitha's statement as she put out some dried fruit and seeds for her pet. She watched the bird pecking at its food and thought about how it was able to imitate so many sounds. Perhaps she *had* been placed in this area for a specific purpose. If that were the case, she needed to be ready to answer God's call, whenever and wherever she could.

Hope bloomed anew and she smiled as the mockingbird finished eating and began its song once more.

eight

Jared tapped the end of his pen on his notebook and considered how to end his exposition. He wanted it to be perfect. He would be presenting it at the meeting next week.

He glanced out the window toward the Tennessee River and watched as a boat floated swiftly past the college. Traffic had dwindled over the past months, not because of the weather but because of the war. He didn't know of any blockades along the river, but the Unionists were curtailing trade with Europe by blockading ports along the East Coast. Many cotton growers were already concerned as they watched the demand for their goods diminish. Cutting off funds for the Confederacy was a solid strategy and one that he applauded as it minimized bloodshed and the need for neighbors to continue fighting and killing each other.

The door to his room swung open, and Benjamin stomped in, so covered by a woolen scarf that Jared had to look twice to identify his roommate. "Is it getting colder?"

"It feels like the rain might turn into snow at any minute." Benjamin pulled off his scarf and shook it several times to remove excess water.

"Hey." Jared held up his arm to shield his paper. "Be careful with that. You're going to ruin all my hard work."

"What are you working on there?" Benjamin pulled off his greatcoat and laid it across the back of a chair.

Jared carefully mopped up the stray droplets threatening

his paper. "It's a treatise on the barbarity of slavery."

Benjamin whistled. "I hope you're not planning to give that to Mr. Whitsell. He's not partial to Union sympathizers."

"It's for the Philomathesian Society meeting." Jared stood up and yawned, stretching his arms to work out the kinks from sitting stooped at his desk for too many hours. "Remember I told you I joined and I've been placed on the program. You are still planning to attend, aren't you?"

"Of course." Benjamin slapped him on the back. "I wouldn't miss it for the world."

"And you promise not to laugh, right?"

"Now, I don't remember agreeing to that." Benjamin ducked a fake punch that Jared threw. "Hey, save your moves for the war."

"Where have you been?" Jared sat back down and held his cold hands close to the oil lamp on their shared study desk. The steam pipes bringing heat to their room clanged and hissed, but they did little to dispel the chill in the room.

"Artillery practice."

"Aren't your hands freezing?"

Benjamin nodded. "Why don't we go downstairs and sit by the fire for a while. A bunch of fellows are down there right now. One of them has a brother who's a member of the Fighting 8th." His voice was filled with reverence for the Georgia regiment that had fought hard in the battle of Manassas plain and suffered the loss of many of its veteran soldiers. "His brother has written a long letter, and Tom's promised to read it to whomever wishes to attend."

"I don't think so." Jared was interested in hearing about the war, but he really needed to concentrate on his project. It had to be the best thing he'd ever written. When he read this out loud to his peers, he wanted to see the fire of righteousness enter their eyes. He wanted them to stand and cheer. He wanted to be the hero, challenging their preconceptions and conquering their stubbornness. In short, he wanted to win the war without firing a single shot. "I have some more work to do."

He could feel the weight of Benjamin's gaze on the back of his neck, but Jared refused to turn around. After several seconds, he heard the door open and close.

He breathed a sigh of relief and reread his last sentence. He needed something extraordinary for a rousing finish. In his mind's eye he could see the scene. The president of the society had told him ladies would be present. Hopefully, none of them would swoon over the power of his words.

He wondered if the editor who'd been at last week's lecture would attend. His heart beat faster. Maybe the man would offer him a job on the spot. How exciting it would be to use his talents to educate and awaken the population. Everyone knew the city had many Union sympathizers. If he was hired on by Mr. Stone, he could really make a difference. It had always been his dream to use his talents for good. This might be his chance.

Jared leaned back in his chair and closed his eyes. He would send a copy of his first newspaper cover to his parents. The great Adam Stuart would be impressed by his son's achievements. And Ma would tell all her friends about her famous son.

He would be working for the downtrodden without having to spend all his time with his nose stuck in dusty law books. He would be the voice of the oppressed, the man whose uncompromising honesty brought peace to his countrymen— all of them, regardless of the color of their skin.

He smiled. All he had to do was finish. He opened his eyes

and dipped his pen in the inkwell. The words flowed again.

❧

Amelia glanced over at Luke Talbot, sitting so straight on his stallion. The sunlight made his dark hair shine. She put a hand to her own head and tugged on the red cap that matched the braided coat of her riding habit. "Do you think my kepi is too daring?"

Luke's smile eased her fears. "You look dashing. I'm sure all the other ladies are quite put out that their own hats are so old-fashioned. They will probably rush out to purchase an ensemble exactly like the one you're wearing."

"You are very kind, Luke. You always know just what to say."

"And you are a delightful companion." He tossed her a look full of meaning but was interrupted by someone calling out from a carriage traveling toward them.

The bright yellow landau was occupied by a pair of ladies who looked familiar, although Amelia couldn't quite recall their names. The older lady waved her lace handkerchief at them as the coachman brought the carriage to a stop.

Amelia and Luke also brought their horses to a halt as Amelia searched her memory. She put on a bright smile and waited for the lady to speak. Perhaps it would come to her, or maybe the passengers themselves would give her a clue as to their identities.

"Good day, Miss Montgomery. What a pleasure to see you about." The lady pointed her fan at the young lady sitting opposite her. "Faye was only this morning asking if we could pay you and your sweet aunt a visit."

"My aunt and I would be delighted to receive you Mrs."— Amelia dredged the name up from her memory—"Downing. And I look forward to renewing my acquaintance with Faye."

Mrs. Downing nodded and turned her attention to Luke.

"Mr. Talbot, isn't it? I trust you are enjoying your studies."

Luke bowed over the lady's proffered hand and murmured an agreement. "How kind of you to remember me."

"Oh yes." Mrs. Downing glanced toward her daughter. "Faye never forgets a face. And her father and I are staunch supporters of the university you are attending. We have a son who will most likely go to school there one day."

Luke assumed an interested expression and nodded. He did not seem eager to continue the conversation.

Mrs. Downing looked from him to Amelia and smiled. "I should be letting you young people get back to your ride. Faye and I will be stopping by this afternoon. I have something of great import to discuss with you, my dear."

Amelia didn't know how to take the woman's statement or the meaningful look that accompanied it. Perhaps she wanted Amelia to befriend her daughter. Maybe Faye wished to secure Benjamin's attention. She smiled at the younger woman and was rewarded by a smile that made her think of an eager puppy's. That must be it. She watched as Mrs. Downing sat back against the cushioned seat and gestured to the driver.

"The park is growing crowded." Luke's voice brought her attention back to the present. He loosened his horse's reins and moved forward.

As she followed her escort, Amelia took note of the dozen or so carriages trundling along the pathway that wound through tall trees and along the banks of the Tennessee River. They moved slowly to allow for conversation. "Yes. It's amazing. I didn't realize quite how popular this park would be."

Luke glanced at her. "There's no reason why you should. It's not like you've spent any time in society."

Amelia didn't know whether or not she should be offended by his remark. Was Luke calling her a rustic? Yet how could she take offense when that's exactly what she was? The safest thing to do would be to introduce a new subject. "Have you seen my cousin lately?"

"He was on the parade ground yesterday evening." Luke's chin rose a notch. "He's going to make a fine soldier."

"Please don't say anything about that to my aunt. She's fearful he will join the campaign and end up wounded or dead."

"Would she rather he take the coward's way out by not enlisting? I think his parents should applaud his patriotism. He and I both share the desire to fight for our principles. Someday I hope we will be comrades in arms. Your aunt is not a traitor to the Confederacy, is she? I know many such reside in Knoxville, but I had not thought to find them within your family."

Amelia's face grew hot under his stare. She didn't know which way to look. What if Luke knew the truth? She was the one who was helping slaves escape north. Would he also condemn her and the actions she took? The answer was obviously yes. He might even feel it his duty to report her to the authorities.

"I cannot imagine anyone in my family sympathizing with the abolitionists." The lie tripped off her tongue easily, and her conscience stung her for a brief moment. Then the thought came to her that she had to deceive Luke or lose her ability to help those poor men and women. "Uncle Francis supports the rights of states to make their own decisions without federal interference."

"Quite right. As do I." Luke reached over and captured her hand in his. "And I know you and I agree on the issue of slavery."

Luke had no idea how she felt about slavery. He had just confessed his desire to fight for the South in support of his principles and expressed his disdain for "traitors to the Confederacy." He must believe she viewed slave labor with the same complacency as her father. Was it wrong for her to be relieved he had accepted her lies? Again her conscience prodded her, but this time, Amelia easily smothered it. She hadn't meant to become involved with the Underground Railroad, but since she had, it was essential that she mask her true feelings.

Luke's mount reared onto his hind legs. Amelia watched in admiration as he kept his seat and brought the horse under control. He looked so capable and strong. She might not agree with him in all areas, but she knew Luke Talbot was a good man. Her heart warmed as she saw her lifelong friend in a different light. He was no longer the mischievous young man who'd teased and played with her while their parents visited in the parlor downstairs. Luke was a grown man, and one who could probably set female hearts fluttering all over Knoxville. Gratitude for his attention warmed her.

She sent him a challenging look as he subdued his horse. "Perhaps we should try a gallop." Without waiting for an answer, she clucked at her mare.

Luke was only a second behind her, his stallion's longer legs eating up the distance between them. Then they were riding neck and neck, their horses straining to reach the line of trees in the distance.

Amelia's kepi caught the wind and lifted from her head, so she had to draw in the reins and drop out of their impromptu sprint. She turned her mare's head around and spotted the red cap on the ground some feet back. She would have to remember to ask Tabitha to secure it more tightly in the future.

Hooves thundered behind her. Amelia looked over her shoulder to see Luke racing to the rescue. The wind teased at her hair as he raced past her and dismounted with alacrity. He scooped up the cap and tucked it under one arm. Then he reached for her and swung Amelia out of her saddle, his hands encircling her waist.

Luke was ever mindful of decorum and released her as soon as her feet touched the ground. So why did she feel so breathless? She gazed up into his brown eyes and wondered if the gleam was caused by his usual kindness. Or was there something warmer in his expression? And if there was, how did she feel about that development?

She and Luke had grown up as close as siblings, but if she was reading him right, the emotion he was currently feeling had nothing to do with brotherly affection. Unsure of herself, Amelia stepped back and lowered her gaze to the ground.

"I. . .Amelia, I must admit to an ulterior motive in bringing you out today."

That brought her gaze up again. He looked normal now, the Luke she'd grown up with, the Luke she felt comfortable with. "What is it?"

He cleared his throat. "There is a function at the college next Saturday evening, and I wondered if you would like to attend. . .with me."

"I would be most flattered to have you as an escort, Luke, as long as my aunt and uncle agree."

"Of course." He ran a finger under the collar of his shirt. "It's a rather special affair, a meeting of the university's literary society."

"That sounds nice. Will there be dancing?"

He nodded. "But before that, several writers will take turns reading their works to the audience. My name is on the program."

Amelia clapped her hands together. "That's wonderful. I never knew you were a writer. You must be quite talented."

"I don't know about that. But my literature professor has been very encouraging." Luke's humility was as unexpected as it was pleasant.

Amelia had always thought of him as being self-assured, as in control of his life as he'd been over his mount a little while ago. She was beginning to see the man in a whole new light. One that opened her eyes to possibilities she had never imagined before.

nine

Jared checked his appearance in the mirror one last time.

Benjamin slapped him on one shoulder. "You look quite dapper."

"How does my cravat look?" He patted the starched cloth and turned so his roommate could judge. He held his breath as Benjamin's gaze traveled upward from his feet, checking every detail.

"Not too shabby." Benjamin nodded. "You'll do well."

Jared let his breath escape in a *whoosh*. He was ready if Benjamin pronounced him satisfactory. He reached for his papers. "Are you ready?"

Silence answered his question. Jared returned his attention to Benjamin. His roommate had discovered a sudden interest in his bed pillow.

"Benjamin?"

"I can't come." Benjamin looked up, an unreadable expression on his face.

Jared wanted to protest. His closest friend wouldn't be there? "I thought you wanted to open a newspaper with me."

"I know, I know." Benjamin jammed his hands into his pants pockets. "And I do. But I just don't feel like getting out. It's been a hard afternoon."

"What do you mean?" Thoughts about the evening were whisked away as Jared considered Benjamin's words. Several things that he'd ignored while working on his magnum opus came to mind now. The amount of time his roommate had spent on the parade grounds. The studies he was ignoring.

As he'd wrestled with phrasing and grammar, a part of Jared had wondered how Benjamin ever expected to catch up with his classwork, but he'd been far too busy to ask many questions. Now guilt attacked him. What kind of friend was he?

"I've been down to Gay Street."

Benjamin's words did not sink in at first, but then he knew. His friend had visited the enlistment office.

"Did you enlist?" The three words fell between them.

Benjamin pulled his hands from his pockets. He went to the window and stared out at the bleak winter evening. Jared walked over to him and gazed at the bare limbs of the trees scattered across the campus. The silence in the room was broken as a loud banging came from the steam pipes that brought heat into the room. Jared waited. However much time it took, he would wait to hear what Benjamin needed to tell him.

"No. I didn't enlist." Benjamin's voice was so hushed that Jared had to lean toward him.

"You didn't enlist? Why did you go there then?"

"I wanted to enlist. But I kept hearing my ma's sobs and seeing the look of disappointment on Pa's face. So I just hung around for an hour." He looked up, a deprecating grin turning up the corners of his mouth. "How's that for a lame story?"

Jared punched his upper arm. "Sounds more like a son who honors his parents' wishes."

"Trust you to put a good face on it." Benjamin glanced at him. "You don't think I'm a coward?"

"You? A coward?" Jared didn't have to fake the shock he felt. "I think your biggest problem is a tendency to leap before you look. You and I are only freshmen. We should stay in school as long as we can."

"But what if the South wins the war before we graduate? What if we miss our one and only chance to fight for our country?"

Jared could have made several answers. The words burned his throat. Words about the evils of slavery and the overwhelming odds aligned against the Confederate states. But now was not the time to go into that. They could debate the reasons for secession at some other time. They had discussed the subject in the past and would undoubtedly do so again. "I don't think that's going to happen. President Lincoln seems determined to keep fighting for quite some time."

"Well in that case, maybe I do have time to come to your poetry reading." Benjamin pushed an elbow into Jared's side.

Instead of protesting Benjamin's characterization of his serious paper, Jared laughed. "That's good. But you'd better get dressed. There's not much time, and I want to—"

"Get there early." Benjamin finished the phrase for him, and his laughter joined Jared's.

Optimism buoyed Jared. It was going to be a great evening.

❧

Amelia settled into the carriage and touched the fur collar of her pelisse with a gloved hand before burying her cheek into its softness. She smiled at Tabitha, her chaperone for the evening with Luke. "Are you warm enough?"

Tabitha nodded and helped Amelia arrange a blanket over both of their laps. Amelia was so excited she could barely contain herself. She'd never been to a literary society reading and wondered if she would make any new friends this evening. She hoped so. She loved literature and would appreciate having friends with similar tastes.

Luke clambered in and settled in the opposite seat, his back to the coachman. He looked especially handsome this evening, his dark hair curling onto his high forehead. She would be the envy of the other women in attendance.

"You look lovely, Amelia." His deep voice filled the tiny space. He reached forward and took one of her hands in his. "I am so glad you were able to join me."

"Me, too." She pulled her hand free when Tabitha cleared her throat. The coach moved forward, and she settled back for the ride across town. "Please tell me what to expect tonight, Luke."

She sensed rather than saw his smile in the dark carriage. "It should be interesting. Several of the freshmen have written essays. They were visited by one of our local newspaper editors, and I understand that he inspired the whole class."

"Will my cousin be there?"

"His name is not on the program, but I believe he may attend since his roommate, the young man we met on the train, will be presenting a work. And I've already told you that I'll be reading a poem."

Amelia heard the rustle of paper.

"Would you care for a preview?"

"I would be delighted, but how can you read in this gloom?"

A chuckle answered her. "I have been reading it again and again ever since you agreed to come with me. I wanted to impress you by reciting it from memory."

"Then perhaps I should wait and be impressed with the rest of those in attendance."

"As you wish." The paper rustled once more as Luke apparently tucked it into his coat pocket.

"Are you going home for Christmas?" Amelia was excited about the upcoming holiday even though it was still two months away. She and Aunt Laura had already begun to consider the decorations. Of course, it was too early to bring in a Christmas tree, but they had already begun stringing berries and raisins for garlands and stitching bits of lace and ribbon to baskets that would be filled with fresh fruit for the holiday. They had pored over decorating ideas from previous issues of *Godey's Lady's Book* and discussed several intriguing projects.

"I don't know. There's talk of the school closing early because of the war."

Amelia could feel her eyebrows rising. She had not heard of this. "I didn't know. But the atmosphere in Knoxville does seem to be getting more tense. Yesterday when Tabitha and I were shopping for holiday ribbon, we saw soldiers marching through the streets. They seemed so serious, all stepping in time and holding their weapons on their shoulders. I am planning on attending a rally tomorrow."

"I don't know if that's wise, Amelia." She could hear the hesitation in Luke's voice. "It might be a good idea for you to plan to return to your parents. I don't think things are nearly so unstable in Nashville. Knoxville is a target for both sides because of the two rail lines that intersect here."

She didn't know how to answer him. She doubted her papa would welcome her return. He'd made it very clear that she was to stay in Knoxville for at least a year. She was saved from coming up with a reply by their arrival at the college.

Luke opened the door and disembarked before turning to help her as she followed him. She stepped aside, expecting him to offer the same assistance to Tabitha, but Luke slipped a hand under her arm and led her away from the carriage. "What about our chaperone?" Her voice gently chided him for his insensitivity.

"She'll be fine."

Amelia halted, forcing Luke to do the same. "I insist."

An exasperated sigh answered her, but he let go of her arm and turned back to help Tabitha alight. His grip was not as gentle when he returned to her, but Amelia didn't care. She would not stand for her friend to be treated with disdain, and if Luke didn't like it, he was not the man for her.

❧

Jared rose from the folding chair and bounded up the steps to the stage. He cleared his throat and looked at the sheet of paper in his hands. His palms were sweating, and his spectacles slipped. He settled them more firmly on the bridge of his nose and cleared his throat again. A quick prayer for courage resulted in a measure of confidence. It was time for his star to rise.

He began to read, his voice rising and falling as he described the injustices of slavery—the horror of being owned by another, the tragedy of losing children and spouses who were sold to other owners, and the indignity of having no control over the least aspects of one's daily life. The audience grew restless as he described life from a slave's point of view. He was not surprised. Most of the people in attendance tonight, if not all, owned slaves. But he would not apologize for his words. They were true. Harbingers of the future. He prayed some of those in the audience would be open to his message.

When he finished, the applause could only be described as sparse. He returned to his chair and relaxed, glad to have his public reading finished. Now he could look forward to some lively dialogue about the issues he'd raised.

The next student headed for the stage, but Jared was still energized from his experience on the stage so he barely heard a word. He considered the audience. He had not been surprised to see Luke Talbot in attendance. The man was a member of the society. But his companion had shocked Jared.

Amelia Montgomery. He'd spotted her as soon as he reached the stage. Who could not see her effervescent beauty even in a roomful of people? She would stand out in any crowd. Yet she seemed so kind and unassuming. He thought of their conversation during her birthday celebration. During that admittedly brief interlude, she had managed to make him feel as if he was the very center of her attention.

Did she and Luke have an understanding? It seemed likely since he was her escort once again.

As he was about to turn away, she glanced up and their gazes locked. Jared could hardly remember to breathe. Then Luke leaned over her and whispered something in her ear. The distraction made her look away, and Jared realized in that moment that he had better stay far away from Amelia or risk losing his heart.

The readings ended. An orchestra took over the stage, and the audience began to mill around, renewing acquaintances and discussing the presentations. The floor was cleared of the chairs for dancing.

Jared didn't plan it, but somehow he ended up shoulder to shoulder with Amelia. He knew it when her perfume tickled his senses. He tried to move away, but the press of the crowd prevented it.

"Good evening, Mr. Stuart." Her voice was calm, self-assured. "I enjoyed your essay immensely."

Jared could feel his ears heating up. They were probably as red as hot coals. He noticed Amelia's fuchsia-colored dress. Several satin ribbons scattered across it, along with rosettes that matched the color of her velvet gown. He noticed that the sleeves were wide and full at the elbows but wrapped snugly around her slender wrists. She was wearing a double strand of pearls, and a pearl comb was perched at the crown of her head.

"Hello." It was the only word he could squeeze out of his tight throat. Again, he wondered what she was doing here. Benjamin hadn't mentioned anything about her attendance. Why hadn't he warned Jared about the possibility? Hadn't he visited with his family last weekend? Jared could distinctly remember turning down an invitation to join him for Sunday dinner. Perhaps he should have accepted as he would have at least been prepared to see her tonight.

"Yes, who would have thought of taking the viewpoint of the slaves?" Luke Talbot's words had a rough edge that bespoke his disdain.

Jared could feel his ears again. They were going to burst into flame at any moment.

"I thought it was inspired." Amelia's eyes, as blue and clear as the summer sky, caught his attention and held it. "You are a talented writer." He felt her hand on his arm.

He wished he was as good with the spoken word. "Thank you." Jared knew he needed to get away from this corner of the room. Get away from her so he could think again. "Would you care to dance?" Had those words come from his mouth?

Apparently so, as Amelia nodded. "I'd love to."

Jared led her to the center of the dance floor. "I didn't have any idea you would be in attendance this evening." He winced. He sounded callow. Next he would be talking to her about the weather.

"I am so glad I was able to hear your piece especially, Mr. Stuart." Her smile warmed his ears once more.

"I cannot imagine that you agree with anything I wrote."

She bit her lip for a moment, looking adorable as she considered how to answer him. "Whether I agree is not the point. I doubt you intended your words to be heard only by abolitionists. Wasn't it your intention to make all your listeners think of slavery in a different light?"

She understood. Jared could no longer feel the floor beneath his feet or hear what anyone else said. The whole of reality shrank down to the two of them. They might have been standing in the middle of a busy street or on the moon. Her expression told him she was speaking from the heart. He would have been happy if the moment could have continued for an eternity. Just the two of them, so close in body, mind, and spirit.

The orchestra ended the song, but Jared did not want to let go of her. He hated to surrender Amelia to her escort, but the rules of society demanded it. She stepped back from the circle of his arms. Was she blushing? His heart pounded. He opened his mouth to say something but halted when Luke walked up and whisked her away. She glanced over her shoulder at him once before being swallowed up by the crowd.

He had no memory of leaving the dancers, but he must have because he found himself standing in a group of his classmates. They were discussing the war, of course. It was the topic that seemed uppermost in everyone's mind. Jared smiled or frowned as necessary, but his thoughts were still on the way Amelia had reacted to him, the way she had fit so well in his arms.

"It looks like the evening met your expectations." Benjamin clapped him on the shoulder. "I saw you dancing with my cousin. Should I inquire as to your intentions?" A laugh followed his teasing remark.

Jared shook his head. "I doubt she remembers who I am."

"I don't know about that. She seemed content to let you lead her around the dance floor, yet I noticed that few others of our friends got the same honor."

"Luke danced with her several times." Jared could have bitten his tongue off as soon as the words were out of his mouth. He escaped the ballroom, Benjamin's knowing laughter trailing him. As he gathered his hat and coat, he wondered how he could have been so foolish as to let anyone know he'd been watching Amelia that closely.

Lanterns from the guests' coaches lighted the pathway to the dormitory. Jared relived the evening in all its glory—the applause, the accolades of his classmates and professors, and the admiration in a certain pair of blue eyes. Had he found his calling? Had God given him the talent and opportunity to make a difference?

Pushing back his confused feelings about the beauteous Amelia, words of thanksgiving and praise filled his heart, and his feet seemed to have grown wings. He could hardly wait to get back to his room and begin writing his next opus.

ten

Amelia gathered her medicines together and headed downstairs. Tabitha had told her that another group of slaves had been brought in and were resting in the barn as before, and she knew she would not be able to get a wink of sleep until after she checked on them. She pushed her bedroom door open and crept down the stairs, thankful for the dim glow of a lantern that showed her the way to the kitchen.

All the dishes and leftover food had been stored, and the fire was banked for the evening. She shivered and pulled her cloak tighter around her shoulders. A squeaky noise behind her made Amelia freeze and hold her breath. After a moment passed without further noise, she eased forward once again.

She opened the back door and slipped through it, picking her way along the path to the barn. She'd been out here several times in the past weeks, even though she had originally hoped her work with runaway slaves would be done after Melek took that first group out of town. But that had only been the beginning for Amelia, the agent Melek now referred to as the Mockingbird.

She stopped outside the door and pursed her lips. Her first attempt at a whistle failed miserably, sounding more like a hissing snake than a bird. Amelia licked her lips and tried again. There! That was more like it. She was quite proud of the liquid sound she produced.

After a moment, the barn door opened, and the old

coachman, whose name she had learned was Tom, grinned at her and beckoned her inside. He led the way to the tack room. "We've a tired group tonight. They been running for days without much sleepin'."

Amelia went inside, and her heart melted at the sight that met her eyes. A couple about her own age cowered against the wall. The young man had a protective arm about the girl. He watched Amelia with wary eyes.

"I came out here to help you." She set her bag of medicines down on the floor and dropped to her knees beside them. "Let me see your feet."

She unwound several layers of dirty cloth from the young woman's feet, dismayed to see the cuts and bruises on them. It was a good thing she had found a merchant who sold tincture of iodine. She soaked a clean length of cotton in the solution and gently cleaned the young woman's feet. Tearing several new lengths from a discarded sheet she had rescued last week before it could be thrown away, she rewrapped the slave's feet before turning to her companion.

"You have a gentle touch." The young man's eyes were not nearly as wary as they had been before.

"I need to do the same for you."

He nodded and stretched out his feet, and Amelia began the process again. When she finished, she drew out some of her precious willow bark. "If you chew on this while you are walking, it should ease your pain."

The young woman reached out her hand and took the bark from Amelia before settling back into the curve of her husband's arm.

"Where are you from?"

"Al—"

"It's safer if you don't know too much, miss." Tom the

coachman interrupted the girl before she got more than the first syllable out.

Amelia's cheeks heated as she glanced at the old man. "You're right. It's not the time for polite conversation."

Amelia gathered up her supplies, pointing to the bloody rags she had removed. "Those should be burned. They are too dirty to be of use to anyone."

"I'll take care of it." The old man held open the door to the tack room. "It's time for you to get back to the big house."

It was nearly dawn by the time Amelia divested herself of her clothing, her mind on the frightened pair hiding out back. They had so far to travel on their poor feet. She hoped her ministrations would help speed their journey. As she drifted toward sleep, Amelia prayed for their safety and for the courage to continue helping those like them.

❧

Sunshine warmed Amelia's face as she stood amongst the crowd. She was frustrated at not being able to see the foot soldiers, but at least she could hear the cadence of the drums and the reedy notes of the fifer. The mounted cavalry looked smart in their matching, double-breasted frock coats, gray in color with gold buttons and red silk sashes. Given the way Luke had talked last week, he would soon be one of them. She could imagine him sitting proudly astride, his shoulders straight and his red forage cap, so like the one that went with her own riding suit, perched on his dark hair.

The people around her seemed to be caught up in the patriotism of the day. They cheered and waved. Some of the ladies even blew kisses to the men in the parade. The horses were barely past her location in the crowd when Amelia spied two flags—the first was the Bonnie Blue flag, a single white star in a field of brilliant blue. Following it was the official flag of the Confederacy, a bright white stripe separating two red stripes and a circle of stars inside the blue corner on its upper left side. Luke had told her a different flag, the Southern Cross, led soldiers on the battlefield. The colors of this flag reminded her of the Union flag, but the differences it symbolized opened a pit of despair in her stomach.

She supposed the soldiers must be marching behind the flags, but all she could see were the tips of their bayonets. A young boy wove in and out of the crowd, following the progress of the soldiers. A miniature drum was slung over his shoulders, and he beat a tempo to match that of the parade drummers. She wondered where his parents were. If they were not careful, the child was likely to become the youngest member of the army, judging from his fervent expression.

"Miss Montgomery, Miss Montgomery." The sound of someone calling her name took Amelia's attention away from the youngster. She turned and recognized Mrs. Downing.

"I am so happy to find you, Miss Montgomery." Mrs. Downing was out of breath from pushing her way through the crowd of onlookers. "Your aunt said you had planned to attend the parade."

"Hello, Mrs. Downing." She looked behind the older lady, searching for Faye, but could not spot the tall, spare girl. "Where is your daughter today?"

"She is. . .indisposed this morning." Mrs. Downing looked around them. "Can we go somewhere to talk?"

"I am sorry to hear that." Amelia gestured Tabitha toward them. "Where would you like to go?"

"There's a house about a block from here which is being used as a church and for other, more important purposes." Mrs. Downing's glance was pregnant with a meaning that escaped Amelia. She grasped Amelia's arm and began pulling her away from the other spectators.

Mrs. Downing loosened her grip as the crowd thinned. The soldiers were more than a block away by now, the sound of their marching feet fading into the distance. Finally Mrs. Downing, Amelia, and Tabitha came to a street corner. A two-story frame house stood there, its windows boarded up, its doors scarred as though from fire or assault. Their guide hesitated before going up to the door, and she looked around once more before turning and gesturing for Amelia and Tabitha to follow her. "Come on. We'll be able to talk inside." She pushed open the front door.

Amelia heard it squeal in protest. "Whose house is this?"

"The original owners are not important. The only thing that matters is that it was donated to the free blacks they had employed and now has new life as a church." Mrs. Downing led them past an empty parlor and several closed doors toward the back of the house where the original kitchen would be. She pushed open the door.

The sight that met Amelia's eyes caused her to halt. Several battered trunks sat on the floor, their lids open. They were filled with clothing—skirts, trousers, shirts, and hats. The far wall was lined with shoes and boots, neatly arranged in order of size. Jars of preserved foods lined the shelves, and a pile of blankets lay neatly folded on a large table. Nothing was new, but the room held more items than any mercantile she had ever shopped.

Her gaze met Tabitha's in wonder before she turned back to Mrs. Downing. "What kind of place have you brought us to?"

The older woman's wave encompassed the items. "It's a storeroom. It has been filled by people who disagree with the position of our great state, people who are sympathetic to the plight of slaves, people who believe slavery must end if our country is to survive."

Amelia could feel Mrs. Downing's gaze on her. "How do you know I will not turn you in to my aunt and uncle?"

"Because you are the Mockingbird, the person responsible for helping more than one group of slaves escape capture."

A tall black man stepped through the servants' entrance into the kitchen. He was dressed in a loosely cut, brown frock coat, fawn-colored trousers, and a brown silk brocaded waistcoat.

Amelia did not recognize him until Tabitha breathed his name. "Melek!"

He nodded to her before turning to answer Amelia's question. "Mrs. Downing is a friend of mine. I asked her to bring you to me." He then turned his smile on Tabitha. "You are surprised to see me, little one?"

Tears pooled in Tabitha's eyes as she nodded. "You look so. . ."

He tugged at the cuff of his sleeve. "Civilized is the word I think you seek."

"I was going to say handsome." Tabitha put a hand to her mouth, apparently as shocked as Amelia at her forwardness.

Amelia watched as his smile broadened. He bowed over Tabitha's hand. "These clothes are what I wear when I am not in the South. But when I leave this church, I will once again don the ragged clothing of a slave."

"It matters not to me what clothing you wear."

Feeling like an eavesdropper, Amelia cocked her head toward the front of the house, and she and Mrs. Downing left the couple alone.

"I'm sorry there's no furniture." Mrs. Downing stepped into the parlor and looked around. "It's been sold for clothing, food, and money for the railroad."

"Tell me what you do."

Mrs. Downing chuckled. "They call me a stationmaster. We take all of our terms from the railroad business. Melek is a conductor. He infiltrates plantations and talks to the slaves, offering them his guidance if they wish to escape. I find safe shelter for groups who come through this part of Tennessee."

Amelia watched her closely, admiration overcoming her for this kind woman with unsuspected depth of purpose. "But how do you do it? How do you hide your true nature all the time? Does your family know what you're doing, or do you have to lie to them?"

"I was raised to believe people were equal regardless of the color of their skin, but the man I married does not share my views." She turned from Amelia and walked toward the empty fireplace. "He's a good man, but he does not understand his wife's liberal ideas. So we agree to disagree. I do what I can, provide money and shelter when necessary. He may have some idea about what is going on, but he doesn't ask questions."

Was Amelia looking at her own future? Her heart was heavy. She could not imagine such a thing, yet what was the alternative? Was she destined to be like the mockingbird Melek compared her to, changing her tune all the time to hide her true feelings? She could not turn a blind eye to the injustices around her, but what did God expect of her? What was a conscientious Christian supposed to do?

"I've been working with the railroad for almost two decades now." The older woman sighed. "It's become a way of life for me. Sometimes it does become a heavy burden, but then I receive a message from a grateful family who has been reunited through the railroad's efforts, and I realize how important this mission is."

Amelia listened as Mrs. Downing described the people, young and old, who had passed this way over the years. How could she begrudge sacrificing a few of her comforts for such a worthy goal? The answer was simple. She could not. No matter what it cost, the Mockingbird would have to continue her work.

❧

Jared's stomach grumbled as he sat and listened to the professor droning on and on about Latin declensions. As much as he enjoyed language arts, he could not find anything of value in learning a language that was seldom used for anything other than scientific purposes. Most classical texts had been translated to English, so why should he bother to fill his head with unnecessary drivel? His conscience pricked him at the thought. The university president didn't think it was drivel. Who was Jared to decide which classes were useful?

Another grumble. He glanced around to see if anyone else could hear his protesting stomach. He should have found time for breakfast this morning. But after chapel, he'd been struck with inspiration and hurried back to his room to jot the ideas down before classes started.

Finally, Professor Wallace pulled out his pocket watch. "If there are no questions, we will end today's lesson."

Jared gathered his papers, careful not to let the professor see the drawings he'd created when he should have been taking notes. He folded them into his textbook and put his pencil in the pocket of his waistcoat.

"Be prepared for a test on Friday," the old man continued, raising his voice above the noise of the students who were preparing to leave.

A collective groan answered his announcement. Mr.

Wallace grimaced and turned toward the blackboard, erasing his work in preparation for his next class.

Jared hurried out of the room with the other students, intent on reaching the dining hall and appeasing his stomach.

"Mr. Stuart." A voice called his name, halting Jared's headlong descent down a flight of stairs.

His eyes opened wide. He recognized the short, large-bellied man who stood on the second-floor landing. Martin Stone! The editor of the *Tennessee Tribune*. And he had called Jared by name! Excitement replaced his hunger.

"Mr. Stuart," the editor repeated. "I'm glad I found you." He held out a pudgy hand and grasped Jared's, pumping it enthusiastically. "I have a proposition for you. Actually a job if you're as talented as your professor tells me."

Jared's stomach clenched. A real newspaper editor wanted to talk to him? It was a dream come true. The answer to a prayer. He could feel the grin that stretched his mouth wide. "You want to hire me?"

Mr. Stone returned his grin. "Is there somewhere we can go to talk?"

"I was on my way to the dining hall. Would you care to join me there?"

A shake of his head made Mr. Stone's chin wobble. "We need some privacy."

Jared was torn. His belly was as empty as a pauper's purse. But he desperately wanted to hear whatever it was Mr. Stone had to say. His stomach protested loud and long, warming his ears.

Mr. Stone clapped him on the shoulder. "It sounds like you do need to eat. Perhaps you will let me take you to a small establishment a few blocks from here."

They exited the building and walked briskly away from the college. Jared tried to start a conversation, but Mr. Stone was winded from the exercise, so he contented himself with waiting. They reached the restaurant and took off their coats as they were enveloped in warm air and delicious scents. The restaurant was busy, but Mr. Stone managed to procure them a table tucked away in a far corner.

"I recommend the stewed beef with macaroni." The older man tucked a napkin into the collar of his shirt and beamed at Jared. "Not only is it delicious, it is a prompt meal."

Jared nodded to the waiter, who complimented them on their selections before marching toward the kitchen.

"Mr. Stuart," the man began, his voice hushed, "your literature professor forwarded to me a piece you wrote recently."

"Do you mean my treatise—'The Pernicious Effects of Enslavement in the United States'?"

"Yes, it was an outstanding work." Mr. Stone continued for several minutes. "Almost on the same level as Harriet Beecher Stowe's book."

Pleasure at the man's compliments filled Jared's chest. "Thank you, sir. My parents have always been avid protectors of the rights of others. They taught me to put myself in the place of those less fortunate. When I began to consider how it would feel to be owned by another human being, the words seemed to flow."

"If only more people could share your vision."

The waiter returned with two steaming plates of food and a loaf of dark bread. As soon as Mr. Stone blessed their food, Jared dug in with gusto. Silence reigned at the table while both men satisfied their appetites.

"I'd like to offer you a job." Mr. Stone held up a hand to stop Jared from responding immediately. "You need to understand exactly what I'm talking about before you make your decision. I'm not talking about the *Tennessee Tribune*. This is a different paper, one my conscience has prodded me into starting. I have named it *The Voice of Reason*. It will be distributed throughout the city, and I hope it will garner attention from those who oppose the institution of slavery. The work is sometimes dangerous as it does not support the Confederate mandate. I am too old and unfit for soldiering, so I want to use the strengths God blessed me with to make a difference."

"I want to do it." Jared inserted his statement when Mr. Stone stopped to untuck his napkin and lay it next to his plate.

"The pay will be negligible," Mr. Stone warned. "Probably not even enough for room and board."

"The university feeds and houses me."

Mr. Stone smiled. "Ahh, the enthusiasm of youth. It is exactly what my new venture needs. But make no mistake, this is serious business. If we are caught, you will likely be arrested or fined."

Jared heard the warnings, but his mind was busily crafting a new article for Mr. Stone's newspaper. The opportunities were endless. He wanted to get a message across to the families of Knoxville. His fingers itched for paper and his fountain pen. He could see the title spread across the front page of the newspaper. Like Benjamin Franklin, he would write stories that he prayed would live on long after he died. "I'm your man, Mr. Stone."

"That's wonderful news, my boy. Can you have something for me next Wednesday? If that's too soon, I can see about delaying the next edition until the following week."

Jared took a deep breath. "I will have something written by then."

"Excellent."

He wrung Mr. Stone's hand with enthusiasm, realizing he had finally become a man.

eleven

Bumps and thumps pulled Amelia from her dreams. She tried to ignore the noise, snuggling deeper into the warmth of her quilts and squeezing her eyes shut.

She could make out the sound of Aunt Laura asking someone a question. A deeper voice answered. Then footsteps on the stairs. What was going on?

Giving up on slumber, she pushed back the covers and slid her feet into the slippers at the edge of the bed. She pulled her wrapper on and went to the fireplace, reaching for the bellows used to coax heat from the dying embers.

A soft knock on the door was followed by Tabitha's entrance. "I thought all that noise might have woke you up."

"What's going on?"

"It's Master Benjamin. They say his school has closed on account of the war, and he's come home to stay."

Amelia's heart dropped as she realized that Tabitha's news likely meant Jared Stuart would be leaving Knoxville. Would he think to stop by and visit before going home? "I have to get dressed right away, Tabitha."

Tabitha went to one of the clothing trunks and drew out a red and black plaid dress while Amelia bathed her face and hands from the washbowl. The cold water on her cheeks chased away the last remnants of sleep.

It seemed like hours before she was fully dressed from head to toe, but the pendulum clock hanging next to the window indicated only some forty minutes had passed. Finally she was ready, her hair pulled back in a simple knot Tabitha secured with a red ribbon. She checked her collar and cuffs to make sure they were spotless and flew down the steps to the breakfast room. One glance inside, however, and her heart fluttered inside her chest like a startled bird.

He was here! Sitting at the table and partaking of breakfast like a member of the family. Jared must have ridden with Benjamin.

Amelia drew in a deep breath, clasped her hands in front of her, and entered with all the aplomb she could manage. "I see we're entertaining guests this morning." Amelia addressed her aunt, who was sipping a cup of tea.

"Yes, my dear." Aunt Laura put the delicate china in its saucer and waved a hand toward Jared and Benjamin.

Uncle Francis emerged from behind his newspaper. "It seems the university ended their semester early because of the war." He frowned at Benjamin. "Not that I liked your attendance there anyway. The place has turned into a hotbed for Unionist sympathizers and abolitionists."

"Now, Francis." Aunt Laura raised an eyebrow. "Don't get yourself upset. The school is closed, and the boys are here safe and sound."

Amelia sat down opposite Jared and Benjamin. "Hello, cousin, Mr. Stuart."

Benjamin rolled his eyes, apparently inviting her to share his disdain for his father's pronouncement.

She bit back a giggle and turned her attention to Jared. "How long will you be staying with us before you must return to Nashville, Mr. Stuart?"

"It's likely to be awhile. The trains are not running presently."

"What?"

Jared glanced to Benjamin, who confirmed his statement with a nod. "Someone burned all the railroad bridges around town. I assume that's the reason for the increased military presence. I hear General Zollicoffer is fit to be tied. He's increased patrols around town. It won't be long before he finds the perpetrators."

"In the meantime, you're welcome to stay with us." Aunt Laura inclined her head toward Jared. "I'm sure we will enjoy having some company."

Uncle Francis nodded his head, but whatever reply he might have made was lost as a house slave entered the dining room.

"Mr. Luke Talbot is asking if you are at home, madam."

Aunt Laura dabbed at her mouth with a napkin before answering. "Show him in. He must have a compelling reason for visiting this early."

One of the slaves put a plate in front of Amelia, but too much was happening for her to pay attention to food. First Benjamin and Jared, and now Luke. If any more unexpected guests arrived, they would have to move to the formal dining room to accommodate them.

"Now that's a boy who has his head on straight most of the time." Uncle Francis pointed a finger at his son. "You would do well to emulate him."

The door opened once again, and the first thing Amelia noticed was the uniform Luke was wearing. His double-breasted frock coat was belted at the waist and gray in color. A sword was fastened to the belt, and he carried a black hat under his arm. He bowed to the family and took the empty chair next to Amelia. "Thank you for seeing me this morning." His easy smile encompassed the whole room, but somehow Amelia felt it was directed at her. He shook his head when a slave offered him a plate but accepted a cup of steaming, black coffee.

Amelia looked at Jared when he cleared his throat. "When did you enlist?"

"I purchased my commission this morning." He glanced down at the uniform he must have ordered several weeks earlier. "But as you can see, I've been planning to join for some time now."

"Have you received your assignment?" asked Benjamin.

"Yes." He took a sip of coffee before continuing. "I am to be part of General Zollicoffer's senior staff. Even as we sit here this morning, plans are being made to turn our college into a hospital for the wounded and ill. My squad will be moving the wounded from the battlefield to Knoxville for treatment."

Concern put a lump in Amelia's throat and made her stomach churn. "That sounds like a dangerous task."

Luke reached over and patted her hand. "Might I hope your words mean you will be praying for me?"

She pulled her hand away as if it had been burned. Luke was a dear friend, but she had not yet decided if she wanted him to be anything more than that. "I pray daily for all the soldiers—the brothers, sons, and fathers who make up both sides of this dreadful war."

"Your sentiments do you justice," Uncle Francis spoke up, redirecting her attention to the head of the table. "But perhaps you should confine your prayers to the Confederacy and pray that we will soon succeed in our quest for independence from Northern tyranny."

Out of the corner of her eye, she could see Luke and Benjamin nodding their agreement. Jared, however, did not. He took off his spectacles and buffed them against the sleeve of his jacket. By the time he returned them to his nose, the conversation had veered in another direction.

Admiration for him grew stronger within Amelia as their glances collided. Instead of the anger she was expecting to find, given his opposition to slavery, his gaze held a deep sorrow. A sorrow she instinctively understood. It made her think of the sadness Christ had described when He encountered spiritual blindness and ignorance. Regardless of her blood ties, in that moment, she felt closer to Jared than anyone else in the room.

≈

Jared set his Bible down and looked outside. A slight figure in a dark cloak hurried past the library window. Amelia! He wondered what errand had her outside at this early hour. He shook his head. It was not his business to monitor her routine. He had enough to do—like composing riveting articles for Mr. Stone's new paper.

A thrill passed through him as Jared considered God's timing with his new vocation, a vocation that gave him purpose and direction. He had written to his parents to explain why he had not come home now that the school term was over and most of the burned bridges had been repaired. They had encouraged him to keep his job even though he was missed in Nashville. Although Jared missed seeing his family, he was relieved they did not insist on his immediate return since he was not in any hurry to leave Knoxville.

Not only did he love his work for the *The Voice of Reason*, he also enjoyed being in the same household with Amelia. The more he was around her, the more he admired her grace and humility. She was always patient and kind with others and worked hard at such tasks as mending, knitting, and even rolling bandages for wounded soldiers. She never complained even though few social outings for her to attend were held now that the city was under martial law. Her good qualities reminded him of Solomon's description of a good wife in the book of Proverbs. Amelia was, in short, exactly the type of girl he hoped to one day marry.

Jared took a deep breath and turned his attention back to his Bible. In the past weeks, he had formed the habit of starting his day with quiet meditation in his host's library. Generally, Benjamin slept late, the Montgomery ladies went on calls or errands, and Mr. Montgomery left early for his club or work, not to return until the midday meal or even later.

Lord, thank You for watching over this kind family. Help me to show them gratitude and respect for offering me a place to stay during these difficult days. Create in me an encouraging spirit to bring about a softening of their attitudes toward the bondage of other human beings. Help me to speak out for what is right while still respecting their beliefs. Show compassion on the men who have taken up arms for both sides in this war between states. And Lord, please show me how You would use me—should I fight or not? And if You wish for me to bear arms, which side should I champion? Lord, how can I take up arms against my Southern brothers? But I cannot ignore the plight of those enslaved people the Yankees champion. Please give me a clear answer. I want more than anything to follow Your plan for my life. Thank You, Lord, for the blessings in my life. Please watch over my family and protect them from harm. In the name of Christ, Your Son and my Savior, I pray. Amen.

God's peace saturated the very air around him. Jared breathed deep, awe and love filling him. These moments were so special, and he treasured them. He might have sat still in worship for a minute, an hour, or a day. Time had no meaning.

Voices in the hallway were an intrusion, indicating his

private time had come to an end. With a reluctant sigh, he left the special corner he had come to consider his own and walked toward the hall. Before he could reach it, the carved door swung toward him and Amelia Montgomery, divested of her cloak, stepped inside.

"Oh, excuse me." Her hand went to her mouth when she saw him in the library. Her beauty nearly overwhelmed him. She was wearing a forest green dress with a wide skirt that swayed gently even after she stopped walking. "I was looking for Benjamin. Have you seen him?"

Jared took out his pocket watch and glanced at it. "At this time of the morning, I would guess he's still abed."

A frown wrinkled her brow. "You're probably right. Perhaps I'll borrow something to read and wait for him to make an appearance."

"Mr. Montgomery has an excellent selection." Jared dragged his gaze from her and glanced over his shoulder at the floor-to-ceiling shelves that lined three walls of the room. They were full of an impressive collection of books—from furniture making to lyrical poetry.

"Yes, this is my favorite room in the whole house." She clasped her hands in front of her and looked down demurely, her whole posture one of sweet innocence. "But I don't get to spend as much time here as I'd like."

Jared nodded, but his mind was more occupied by her beauty than her comment. Amelia's golden hair reflected the sunshine streaming through the library window. If she'd been dressed in white, she would probably have been mistaken for an angel.

Her blue eyes, sparkling with the depth and beauty of a perfect diamond, bathed him in appreciation. He felt like a bird soaring above the earth. He reined in his emotions with an effort. "Were you looking for anything in particular?"

She shook her head. "Do you have a suggestion?"

It was no wonder Amelia was so popular. Who could resist her beauty and grace? And she seemed to value his opinion.

The door to the library had been slightly ajar, but now it swung open farther, and Benjamin entered. He was dressed for an outing in a brown suit, his pants tucked into his boots and a low-crowned felt hat in his hand. "Good morning, Amelia. Have you seen Jared this morning?"

"Yes." She made a quarter turn and swept her hand back toward where Jared stood near the bookshelves. "You have found him."

Benjamin's eyebrows climbed toward his hair as he looked from Amelia to Jared. "Am I interrupting?"

Jared's face warmed in response to the speculative glance. "No. In fact your cousin was searching for you and found me instead."

"I see." Benjamin bowed to Amelia. "Did you have an errand for me?"

She dropped a curtsy. "I was wondering if you would escort Tabitha and me to a few stores in town."

His smile disappeared, and Benjamin's brows drew together. "I'm afraid not. I have a pressing appointment that will keep me busy for most of the day. Perhaps tomorrow."

Now it was Amelia's turn to frown. "Or maybe we'll just go alone and not wait for someone to accompany us."

"That's not a good idea." Jared's heart thumped as he stepped between the cousins. Since the burning of the rail bridges, the Confederate Army had increased its presence in the city. "There have been stories in the newspaper of confrontations between soldiers and ordinary citizens. Even the promenades in the park have been halted."

"I will avoid the park." She raised her chin in defiance and continued before either man could remonstrate. "I need to purchase several items for Christmas gifts and decorations. Aunt Laura doesn't feel well, Uncle Francis is at work, and if you are not available, I don't see another choice."

Jared glanced at Benjamin, whose chin was as high as his cousin's. It was easy to see the family resemblance. They both had stubborn streaks as wide as the Tennessee River. "I would be happy to escort you, Miss Montgomery."

Her pert nose lowered a smidgen. "But you are a guest in my uncle's home. I would not presume to impose on you."

"It's the perfect answer." Benjamin grinned at them. "Jared will see you come to no harm, and you can buy all the gewgaws you want." He jammed his hat on his head and hurried out the door.

"If you're sure you don't mind. . ."

Jared thought for a minute of the article he had promised to have finished by this evening. His editor had asked for a piece applauding the brave men and women who risked life and limb to resist the Confederate takeover of Knoxville. It was complete, but he had planned to go over it once more before sending it to his editor. Yet how could he disappoint Amelia? "I'm at your service. When would you like to leave?"

"It will only take me a few moments to get my wrap."

Her open appreciation made him feel like a conquering hero. "I will call for the carriage and meet you in the foyer in fifteen minutes." He followed her out of the library, his feet barely touching the floor as he anticipated the time they would spend together.

❧

"I don't know if the carriage will hold much more." Jared pointed at the small mountain of boxes lashed to the roof and piled in the boot. "We may have to send Tabitha home separately and then get the coachman to come back after us."

"Perhaps you're right, but I am not finished." Amelia reviewed her mental shopping list. She still lacked several items. "There is at least one small purchase I must still make."

He did not groan or even sigh at her pronouncement. Jared Stuart was obviously a patient man. They had visited five different establishments. He had been polite and attentive at each one, but he had grown noticeably more animated while they were at the bookseller's. He had perused the inventory with great interest and discussed several titles with the proprietor. She was glad he'd been distracted there, as it had allowed her to make a special purchase, but she wondered how many more stops he would allow before rebelling.

"What if we send the carriage home and stop for a luncheon before continuing our raid on the local merchants? I know of a quaint establishment not far from here."

She smiled and squeezed his arm. "What a wonderful escort you have been. Far better than Benjamin."

"I have two older sisters who taught me the intricacies of shopping from an early age." He left her for a moment to instruct the coachman. As the carriage rattled off, he returned to where she stood, a warm smile on his face. She liked his smile. It was strong yet gentle, the look of a man of strong principles. And although Amelia wouldn't admit it to anyone, his smile caused a flutter in the center of her stomach.

There was so much to admire about Jared, not the least of which was his willingness to fall in with her plans. As they joked and laughed the morning away, she learned that they shared many of the same convictions.

Walking with Jared to the restaurant he had mentioned, Amelia noticed the gleam from the storefront of a local jeweler. She inclined her head slightly. "What is in that display window?"

Jared drew her closer so they could both see a beautiful display of ladies' brooches, some encased in gold swirls, others surrounded by silver or pearls. Each oval depicted a different subject, although most were portraits of ladies. But Amelia was drawn to one in particular. Its frame was jet black and shiny, but it was the bird painted on the porcelain center that made her look more closely. It was a slender bird with dark gray wings, a white throat, and a light gray head with a sharp black beak. "Look, it's my mockingbird!"

She felt Jared's arm stiffen and looked away from the brooch to see why. He was looking at her like she had grown a second head or something. She had never seen Jared looking so. . .so disgusted. She had thought his eyes were more brown than green, but the sunlight seemed to catch on the green flecks behind his spectacles. Or maybe that was anger. "What has upset you?"

The green in his eyes faded somewhat. "I. . .it's nothing. . . only a difference of opinion."

"What? You don't like the mockingbird brooch?"

He shook his head and pulled her away from the window. "Don't you ever feel sorry for the bird caged in your home?"

She pulled her hand away from his arm. "Sorry? Why should I? The bird seems quite content. He is fed regularly and does not have to worry about being attacked by a hawk or another predator."

Jared sighed. "But does he have the freedom to fly through the forest or watch his nestlings first take wing?"

The question struck her like a runaway carriage. "But if he was so unhappy, would he continue to sing?"

Holding his arm out to her once more, Jared shrugged.

"Perhaps he sings to keep his spirits up."

Amelia allowed him to lead her down the street, her mind chewing on the question Jared had asked. Did she have the right to deny her bird its freedom? Was she as bad as her parents? She accused them of treating others as less important than their own comfort. A small voice whispered in her ear that she was no different. She had caged up one of God's creatures for her own pleasure.

So lost was she in her contemplation that Amelia didn't realize they were being hailed until the Montgomery carriage pulled up beside them. "Whatever is wrong?"

Their coachman, a young man whose shoulders were not nearly as wide as his uniform, looked scared. "They stopped me just up the road, miss."

"Who stopped you?" Jared pushed at his spectacles and glanced back the way the carriage had come.

Amelia looked inside the carriage to make certain Tabitha was not hurt, but it was empty. "Where is Miss Tabitha?"

The coachman raised his arm and pointed behind him. "They said she had no papers—" His voice cracked. "They said she was a wanted woman and they was taking her back to her master in Georgia."

Panic-laced energy flooded Amelia, making her light-headed. "We must rescue Tabitha. She is not an escaped slave." She gripped Jared's arm. "Please, we have to do something."

"Don't worry." Jared's face had turned white, but he managed a quick smile. "No one is going to take her." He helped her into the coach, but instead of joining her on the inside, he climbed up next to the coachman. "Let's find Miss Tabitha."

The coach sped through the crowded street. Amelia grabbed the hanging straps to keep her seat as they bounced through mud holes and swerved to miss oncoming traffic.

Please keep Tabitha safe, Lord. Help us reach her in time. The two phrases echoed over and over again as they searched for the men who had abducted her friend. Stories persisted of bounty hunters who searched for runaway slaves in free states and returned them home to their masters. But Tennessee was not a free state, and Tabitha was not a runaway. If she'd had any idea that bounty hunters were a problem, Amelia would have insisted that Tabitha carry papers of identification on her. But this was the first she'd heard of such an incident. Of course, advertisements for missing slaves were placed in the newspaper on a daily basis, but no one ever seemed to pay them much heed. Especially lately. With the increased military presence, it was terribly ironic that personal safety had lessened.

The pedestrians passed as a blur, but still Amelia searched for Tabitha's face. The cloak she'd worn today was an old one of Amelia's, dark blue in color, with black braiding and large buttons. Amelia's eyes searched frantically. More soldiers than civilians occupied the street, but she still could not spot Tabitha's cloak.

A cry from above alerted her. She prayed one of them had found Tabitha. The carriage lurched to a sudden halt and rocked as Jared leapt from it.

Amelia pushed open the door of the carriage and climbed out clumsily since no one was there to help her alight. She rushed forward to catch up with Jared, her breath coming in gasps.

Two burly men held a frightened Tabitha between them. One was well over six feet tall with bulky arms and a thick chest. The other's weight was almost all contained in his round belly. Both had long, scraggly beards that hid most of their facial features.

"She is not a runaway." Jared was speaking to the taller man. "She belongs to a friend of mine."

"Well, and ain't that lucky." The shorter man spat on the ground and gripped Tabitha's arm more tightly.

"Let go of her!" Amelia flung herself at him and raised her leg to kick him, but she was pulled back by a strong arm. She hit Jared's chest hard enough to see stars.

"You'd better hold on to your little missy." The taller man pulled on his beard with one hand and stared at them. "I wonder how much your wife thinks this gal is worth."

Amelia opened her mouth to correct him but was forestalled when Jared somehow moved her back behind his right shoulder. "Tabitha belongs to this lady."

"I see." The taller one shook Tabitha's arm. "Ya got papers to prove it, missy?"

"My word is good enough, and you know it." Jared's voice was a low growl. "You will release her to me, or we will go to General Zollicoffer and see if he can sort this out."

All the bluster went out of the tall man. He tossed a look at his companion. "I guess we was mistook, Orin. This gal must not be the one we's lookin' fer."

Orin scratched his beard before nodding. He let go of Tabitha's arm.

She pulled away from the taller man and stepped toward them, nearly falling into Amelia's embrace.

"Can you walk, dearest?" Amelia forced the words past the lump in her throat.

A nod answered her.

Then Jared's arm came around both of them, and he guided them back to the carriage. He put Tabitha in first before giving a hand to Amelia. "I'll ride up front and let you two have some privacy."

Amelia touched his cheek with a gloved hand. "Thank you. I don't know what we would have done if not for your fast thinking." She smiled as his face reddened. He was such a good man—kindhearted, strong, smart. If only he had any interest in her. . .

On the way home, Amelia held Tabitha close and stroked her back as she cried into a handkerchief. It was time to send Tabitha north. Jared's words about Amelia's mockingbird came back. Tears came to her own eyes as she considered losing touch with her friend. But it was time to do the right thing. She would make contact with Mrs. Downing and arrange for Tabitha to leave as soon as possible.

Perhaps this was the reason God had let her become embroiled in the Underground Railroad in the first place. Once Tabitha was gone, the Mockingbird would disappear. She would stick to her role as a vapid debutante and sever all ties with the abolitionists.

twelve

Jared dressed carefully for the Christmas celebration. With all the time and energy the ladies had put into it, he had no doubt the evening ahead would be a memorable occasion. A glance in the mirror told him his cravat was straight. He slipped his arms into the navy blue frock coat and tucked a small package into the pocket of his blue silk waistcoat. Satisfied with his clothing, he brushed his hair toward his face, using a bit of pomade to hold it in place. Then he retrieved his spectacles, carefully wiped them clean on a damp cloth, and placed them on his face.

A sigh left his mouth as his reflection became clearer. He would never be as handsome as Luke Talbot or as charming as Benjamin Montgomery. His only talent seemed to lie in writing strong articles. Another sigh filled him. Not a talent to overwhelm the ladies. But perhaps that was best. He had the feeling he would soon be forced to choose a side in the war, and then there would be no time for romance.

Jared left his room and headed down the hall. Anticipation made his steps light. Did Amelia have a gift for him? But why would she? His inability to resist purchasing something special for her did not mean she would have anything to give him.

"Come on down, man." Benjamin beckoned him with an impatient gesture. "We are anxious to see what Amelia and my mother have wrought in the parlor."

Jared hurried down the stairs. "I'm sorry to keep everyone

waiting." A quick glance took in Amelia's ruby red gown. White lace fell from her shoulders to her elbows in three scalloped layers, caught up in the center with a silk carnation. She was standing close to Luke Talbot and conversing with him.

Jared wished he could draw her attention away from Luke. He longed to hold her close and protect her from harm. He remembered how terrified he'd been the day Tabitha had been abducted. If any harm had come to Amelia, he would never have forgiven himself. But even in the tense situation when he'd stopped her foolhardy attack on the bounty hunter, a part of his mind had registered and memorized the feel of her in his arms.

He wondered if she remembered it at all. Sometimes he believed she was warming to him, but then Luke would drop by in his eye-catching uniform and whisk her away to an outing or party. When did the man find time to serve the Confederacy? His eyes narrowed as Luke put a proprietary hand at her waist. Had things progressed so far between them?

Jared grimaced and caught a surprised look on Mrs. Montgomery's face. He stretched his mouth into a smile and bowed in her direction. "Happy Christmas."

She inclined her head. "Happy Christmas, indeed."

"Shall we go in?" Mr. Montgomery offered his hand to his wife.

Jared wished he could escort Amelia into the parlor, but at least Luke had to take his hand away from her waist to offer her his arm. It was small comfort for Jared's envious heart, but his displeasure faded as he and Benjamin followed the two couples into the parlor. The room was awash in the golden glow of candles and the fresh smell of pine. His gaze went to the tall tree that took up the front corner of the room. The angel perched on top of the tree nearly scraped the ceiling. He stepped closer, captivated by the ribbons, candles, and fruit garlands that decorated it.

"Do you like it?"

Jared nodded and turned to Amelia. Her eyes twinkled in the candlelight. "Beautiful." Did she realize he was not only referring to the decorations?

"Yes, indeed." Luke's voice was an unwelcome intrusion. "But I'm not surprised. Your talents have always included making a home cozy."

"It was Aunt Laura's idea." Her voice chided Luke gently, and Jared hid a smile behind a hand.

Mrs. Montgomery joined them beside the tree. "Your modesty becomes you, Amelia, but you are hiding your light under a bushel." She smiled at Luke and Jared. "My niece was the designer. I could never have achieved all of this without her."

Jared shook his head. "Your home is too beautiful and welcoming for me to believe you were not both equally responsible."

"I agree." Amelia linked arms with her aunt. "It took all of our talents to complete this."

Mr. Montgomery poked at the fire and soon had a cheerful blaze going. "Shall we pass out the gifts?"

"Yes, dear." Mrs. Montgomery settled herself on the sofa and patted the space next to her. "Jared, why don't you sit here and tell me about your family's traditions. I'm sure you must miss them very much."

Benjamin and Amelia began sorting the gifts that were piled under the tree and handed them out to the occupants. Everyone had at least one thing to unwrap, even Luke. Jared fingered the sharp corners of the box in his pocket. Would

Amelia like his gift? Was it too personal?

"Here is a little something for you." Amelia held a rectangular package in her hand.

Jared stood up to accept the gift. It was obviously a book. He unwrapped it with a flourish and gasped. It was a first-edition copy of *A Christmas Carol*.

"Do you like it?" Her voice was hesitant.

"Yes, very much." He opened it, his eyes widening when he saw Mr. Dickens's signature. It took him back to the day he'd first met Amelia. "I will treasure it always. It is the perfect present."

"I'm glad." Her stunning eyes twinkled like one of the trinkets on the Christmas tree. "I purchased it that day you took me shopping."

"I have something for you, too." He drew out the small box he'd been carrying and offered it to her.

Her mouth formed an O of surprise as she accepted the box. "What is it?"

"Why don't you sit down and open it?"

He watched a blush rise up to her cheeks. She sat down and carefully pried loose a corner of the brown paper wrapping. Anticipation quickened his pulse. It seemed to take forever, but finally she lifted the top of the velvet box.

"Oooh." Her eyes widened and she looked upward, a wide smile on her face. "Thank you."

Mrs. Montgomery bent toward her. "What do you have, dear?"

"It's a mockingbird brooch." She held the box so her aunt could see it. "One I admired last week when Jared took me shopping."

Luke elbowed him out of the way and bent over Amelia. "I have a Christmas gift I think you'll like." He handed her a large box.

Amelia put the box in her lap while she fastened her new brooch to the collar of her dress. "Thank you, Jared."

Jared felt ten feet tall. He had pleased her. The soft glow in her blue eyes made them appear deeper than ever. He could fall into their depths—so warm, so mysterious. Then she turned her attention to Luke Talbot. She opened her gift, a furry muff, and thanked him sweetly. Jared tried to gauge her pleasure with the second gift. He thought she liked the brooch more.

Soon the other gifts were all opened. He had received socks, a muffler, and a special cleaning solution for his spectacles. He was grateful for the Montgomerys' generosity, but nothing could compare to the book Amelia had given him.

Mrs. Montgomery clapped her hands to get everyone's attention. "Why don't we sing some Christmas carols?"

Her husband grumbled a little, but soon they were all gathered around the large piano. Mrs. Montgomery played, Benjamin turned the pages for her, and the rest of them sang. As his tenor melded with Amelia's soprano, Jared thought maybe this was the best evening of his life.

❧

Luke stood directly behind Amelia, but he was not singing with the rest of them. What was wrong? The other men were singing, although she had to acknowledge the Montgomery men could not carry a tune very well. She wished Luke would relax and enjoy the family entertainment. Out of the corner of her eye she saw Jared singing his heart out. What a difference between the two men.

Her thoughts came to an abrupt halt when Luke tapped her on the shoulder. He inclined his head toward the door and sent her a look. She wondered what he wished to say to her in private. When the song ended, he drew her away with a laughing promise to return her to the festivities after a few moments.

He sandwiched one of her hands with his own. "I am concerned about the closeness growing between you and Stuart."

Amelia's mouth dropped open. He had brought her out here for a lecture? "I don't know what you're talking about."

"Amelia"—his frown was terrible to behold—"he gave you jewelry. And you accepted it."

She fingered the brooch. "My aunt and uncle didn't seem to find the gift improper."

"I'm sure your father would not be as tolerant." He paced the hall with long strides before returning to her side. "I'm not even certain he would approve of Jared staying here with all of you. He's practically branded himself a traitor."

"He's done no such thing." The words rushed out of her mouth in Jared's defense. "You can't believe he's a traitor just because he disagrees with you. He is expressing his beliefs, which I must say come closer to my own than to those of the slave hunters. Don't we have the same freedom of speech as we enjoyed when we were part of the Union?"

Luke spread out his hands, palms up. "I didn't mean to upset you, Amelia. I wanted to warn you to be a little more circumspect."

He wanted what? "My father gave you the responsibility of escorting me to Knoxville, but he didn't give you the right to dictate my behavior."

Instead of answering her right away, Luke reached into his pocket. "Please don't be so angry. I only have your best interests at heart. And to prove it, I have something I want to give you."

With a sense of impending doom, Amelia watched as he

dropped to one knee in front of her. He took her hand in his and pressed a warm kiss on it. She had read about such gestures and knew they should cause a tingle in her spine, or at least in her stomach, but she felt nothing. Nothing but apprehension.

She tried to listen to what Luke was saying. He had an earnest look on his face, and he was going on about his feelings and his duty. "Please say you will agree to marry me before I leave. You'll make me the happiest man in the Confederacy." He stopped talking and lifted the lid on the velvet box.

How she wished it might have been another brooch or a hatpin. . .anything but an engagement ring. But there it was, a golden circle topped by a lovely blue sapphire. "I don't know—" Amelia swallowed hard. Her mind raced around like a mad bee, unable to light on the appropriate response. She knew what her father and mother would say. It was what they'd hoped would be the outcome of her stay with Uncle Francis and Aunt Laura—marriage to someone of Luke's caliber. But could she agree out of a sense of duty? Could she bind herself by oath to a man she did not love?

Or was love something that formed after the wedding? What if she was looking for some giddy happiness that was only a myth? And she had to consider the man kneeling before her. If she didn't agree to marry Luke, would he pine away for her? Hadn't she just heard him say he was leaving? What if she turned him down and he got himself killed for lack of her love? She couldn't bear the thought of being the cause of his death. She found herself nodding her head.

"Really?" Luke pulled the ring from its box and placed it on her finger. "I hope you like the ring. It reminded me of your beautiful eyes."

He stood and pulled her into his arms. Feeling numb, Amelia allowed the embrace. But when she felt him plant a soft kiss on her forehead, she pushed him away. Luke frowned for a moment before relenting. "Let's go in and tell your family."

Her heart thumped unpleasantly in her chest. Did they have to disrupt the festive evening? But delaying the inevitable was senseless. She took a deep breath and nodded.

Luke threw open the parlor doors and pulled her inside. "Excuse us, everyone, but I have an important announcement to make."

Amelia wished she could match his wide smile, but all she could manage was a feeble imitation.

"Amelia has agreed to become my wife."

Aunt Laura squealed and pushed away from the piano. "What wonderful news!" She clapped her hands. "And on Christmas Eve. The two of you will always remember the occasion of your engagement."

Uncle Francis moved forward and slapped Luke on the back. "Well done, my boy. Well done. You've chosen a lovely bride and a good family."

Benjamin echoed his father's sentiments and enveloped Amelia in a brief hug. "You will make a handsome couple."

When she emerged from his hug, Amelia glanced toward Jared. He wasn't saying anything at all. Was his face pale? And what was the flicker of emotion she saw in his eyes before he looked down at the floor. Surely it had not been pain. What did he expect of her? To turn down Luke's offer?

She could not do it. It was fine for Jared to seek a rebellious path—he was a man. She had to live within society's strictures. Her parents had taught her that when they banished her to Knoxville. She was determined to be a dutiful daughter and please them. They had her best interests at heart. Besides, it was not like anyone else appeared interested. For all the men who visited her, Luke was the only one who had asked for her hand in marriage.

Amelia raised her chin and managed to form a slightly more enthusiastic smile. If a certain fastidious student thought she was making a mistake, she would prove him wrong. What did he know about such things, anyway? She would live her life as she thought best.

Her hand reached up to caress the brooch. She was free to make her own decisions.

A small voice whispered a warning in her mind. *You also have the freedom to regret your decisions for the rest of your life.*

thirteen

Amelia stared at the silver tea service, her mind a long way from the chatter in her aunt's parlor. A rustle of skirts brought her head up, and she smiled at Mrs. Downing. The lady and her daughter had become regular visitors to the Montgomery home, although there seemed to be little action on the Underground Railroad. Things had been quiet since the Christmas holidays. Perhaps the January weather was too harsh for runaways to attempt escape.

"You are looking lovelier than ever, Amelia." Mrs. Downing leaned over and patted her hand. "Your betrothal to the handsome Lieutenant Talbot must be putting those roses in your cheeks."

The ladies around her twittered as hot blood rushed to her face. They probably attributed the sight to maidenly modesty. How could they know the true reason behind her discomfiture? Ever since that night, Amelia had felt like a drowning victim. With each congratulatory or teasing remark, the weight of her feelings had dragged her under. She wanted to claw her way to freedom, to give back the sapphire ring on her hand and explain her mistake to Luke. He would understand, wouldn't he?

As if her thoughts had conjured him, the door opened, and Luke stepped into the parlor. Her cousin was close behind him. In the two weeks since Christmas, Benjamin had begun spending most of his time with Luke. It was a development that disturbed her somewhat, but she could do very little about it. She wished Benjamin would spend more time with Jared. Not only were they of an age, she knew she could depend on Jared's common sense to keep Benjamin from joining the fighting.

Luke bowed to Mrs. Montgomery before making a beeline toward Amelia. Just before he reached her, Amelia felt something slide under her hand. A note from Mrs. Downing could only mean one thing—the abolitionists needed her help. She slipped the paper behind the cushion of her chair and rose to meet Luke.

Mrs. Downing sighed and put a hand over her heart. "Ah, young love. How wonderful to see it in the midst of these dreary days."

Luke smiled at the older lady before turning his dark gaze on Amelia. He was every inch the Southern gentleman, from his neatly trimmed mustache and side whiskers to the polish on his boots. He took her hand in his own and raised it to his lips. "I trust you are well, my dear." He squeezed her fingers before letting them go, an indication of his happiness to see her.

Amelia knew her heart should be racing at the display of his affection, but it remained stubbornly calm. "It's nice to see you, Luke."

Behind him, Benjamin cleared his throat to get everyone's attention. "We have news."

"What is it, dear?" Aunt Laura set her cup next to the serving tray.

"Well, you already know the army has taken over East Tennessee University and established a hospital there."

Amelia nodded. Luke had kept them abreast of the activities at the university, and she had read a blistering article in *The Voice of Reason*, an underground newspaper Mrs. Downing had slipped to her just last week. She suspected Jared might have been the author. The article's frank style and uncompromising position matched Jared's personality and reminded her of the paper he had presented during the literary society meeting. She had wanted to quiz him about it, but with the exception of family meals, she had seen little of Jared since Christmas Eve.

She missed the sound of his voice and the way he pushed his spectacles up on his nose when he was thinking. He always listened to her opinions, often engaging in a lively debate.

It would be nice if Luke had time to discuss important issues with her, but he generally treated her like an empty-headed debutante. He was attentive, but if she tried to bring up a serious subject, he told her not to worry about such matters. Perhaps when the war was over, things would be different. They would have more time together, and Luke would pay proper attention to her ideas.

"Luke's skills and knowledge have come to General Zollicoffer's attention. The general is leading his brigade north into Kentucky, but he took time to give Luke here a promotion to captain, and"—Benjamin paused for effect—"the general has given our newest captain a special assignment."

The ladies all crowded around Luke, each clamoring to congratulate him and find out about his new assignment. Amelia hung back. She was worried his promotion would mean he would soon be going into battle. It was bad enough when he was responsible for transporting wounded soldiers to Knoxville. That had been after the battles were fought. This new assignment probably meant he would be in the thick of the fighting. She might not be certain they would make the perfect couple, but she didn't want him to become another casualty.

"The general has put me in charge of finding the traitors who work with runaway slaves. One in particular has been causing a large stir. We recently caught some of the renegades who know him only as the Mockingbird."

Luke's words made her jaw drop. Now her heart was thumping so loud and fast she felt light-headed. She had to get her emotions under control or risk being caught right here in Aunt Laura's parlor.

"Aren't you happy for your brave fiancé?" Benjamin sauntered toward her. His eyes lit on the brooch she often wore, the brooch Jared had given her for Christmas. "Well, look here, Luke. Maybe you should start your investigation with your betrothed." He pointed to Amelia's chest. "Perhaps my cousin is the culprit you seek."

Shocked silence greeted his words. Everyone looked toward her and Benjamin. Amelia did the only thing she could think of. She laughed. It started out somewhat stilted, but the sound immediately eased the tension in the room.

Her cousin's louder and more natural guffaws at his joke reassured the rest of the ladies, who joined in as they realized the improbability of his suggestion.

Aunt Laura shook her head at her son. "You should apologize to your cousin."

"It's quite all right." Amelia was relieved everyone was laughing. It had been a close thing there for a moment. How disastrous it would have been to be unmasked in her aunt's parlor, to be arrested by her own betrothed. She pushed the frightening thoughts back and smiled widely. "I don't mind Benjamin's attempt to bring some lightheartedness to us. We must all learn to take ourselves less seriously if we are to survive this war."

Even as her face showed relaxed mirth, her heart beat a nervous staccato. Was this how her future with Luke would be—always hiding her true self? She longed to allow her heart to fly as free as those she helped escape slavery. . .but she despaired as a door clanged shut on the cage holding her heart.

❧

"What have you done?"

The commotion outside Jared's bedroom broke his concentration. Was that Mrs. Montgomery's voice? He had been answering the letter he'd just received from his parents, but he put down his pen and walked to the door. Then he hesitated with his hand on the knob. He didn't know if he should interrupt or not. It might be a family problem, and no matter that the Montgomerys had opened their home to him, he was not a member of their family.

The voices had moved down the staircase. It sounded like someone was crying. Was it Amelia? Was she hurt? Chivalry filled his chest. He twisted the knob and strode to the head of the stairs.

The Montgomerys—all four of them—were standing in the foyer. Benjamin had his arms around his mother, who was the one weeping. "I am a grown man, and it's about time you stopped treating me like a child." His voice was angry, but he continued patting his mother's back as if to comfort her.

In an instant, Jared grasped the situation. His friend was no longer wearing street clothes. He had donned the gray uniform of the Confederate army. He would be going to war. A stab of concern penetrated Jared's heart. He wanted to add his protest to that of Benjamin's family.

"If you had only come to me, son," Mr. Montgomery's voice was gravelly with pain, "I would have purchased an officer's commission."

"I can stand on my own two feet, Pa."

"As a foot soldier, you'll likely be used as cannon fodder."

Mr. Montgomery's grim pronouncement produced fresh wails from his wife. "Please stop him, Francis. You have to do something."

Jared was about to retreat to his room to keep from intruding, but he must have made some noise because Amelia looked up. Her troubled blue gaze pierced him. She seemed to be pleading with him. But what could he say? No words could undo Benjamin's actions. He had committed to serve the Confederate army. All they could do was pray for his safety.

"Perhaps Mr. Stuart can convince you."

He pushed his spectacles up and took a deep breath before heading down the stairs. "I'm sorry, but I heard a commotion."

Mrs. Montgomery pulled slightly away from her son's shoulder and sent a wobbly smile toward Jared, her eyes red and puffy from her tears. "It's okay, Jared. We consider you part of our family."

"Yes." Mr. Montgomery nodded his agreement. "I never thought I would say this, but I wish my son were as liberal as you. At least your parents don't have to worry about your going off to fight."

Jared wanted nothing more than to return to his room. He felt the same call to arms as his friend. It was hard not to. Most males between the age of fourteen and forty were needed to assure the South's freedom. Freedom. How ironic that Southern leaders sought freedom to determine their own destinies, destinies that relied upon withholding freedom from their slaves.

Benjamin snorted. "You don't have to drag Jared into this.

It's my decision. Besides, I probably won't be gone for long. The officer at the recruiting station has a Bible verse on the wall behind him that reads, 'Five of you shall chase an hundred, and an hundred of you shall put ten thousand to flight.' By this time next month, I'll have whipped so many Yanks, they'll be in full retreat."

Mrs. Montgomery moaned and pulled a handkerchief from the sleeve of her dress.

The words were sheer bravado. The Confederacy could not claim victory based on the Lord's promises to the Jewish people. Jared knew the South was badly outnumbered and had few resources to rely on. Their best hope was to inflict enough pain on the Union so President Lincoln would withdraw his troops and allow the secession to stand. It was a forlorn hope. Allowing the Union to split would make both sides weaker. The whole nation might disintegrate into dozens of independent countries. The vision of the Founding Fathers to create a cohesive power would be lost.

His lack of belief must have shown on Jared's face. His friend turned away from him. "Fine. If you're all against me, I'll get my things together and leave." He took a step back from his sniffling mother and pushed his way past Jared.

Amelia tossed an angry glance at Jared before leading her aunt away. What had *he* done? What did she expect of him? Did she want him to chain Benjamin to keep him here? She would do better to blame her betrothed. Luke Talbot had taken Benjamin under his wing in the weeks since the school closed. Her cousin's decision to join the fighting was probably inevitable. No doubt Luke's influence and success had hastened the event.

Perhaps she blamed Jared for not spending more time with Benjamin. It was true that he'd not spent much time with the Montgomery family since Christmas, but the fault for that lay at her door as much as his. He could not abide the thought of Luke and Amelia together, cooing like doves. So he found reasons either to be out of the house or to be closeted in his bedroom. He felt bad to lose the closeness that had developed between him and Amelia. Her insight and intelligence challenged him to think, but their budding relationship shattered when she chose to link her future to another man.

Mr. Montgomery clapped him on the shoulder. "I'd better go to the bank and buy some of those Confederate notes. Since my son has taken the bit between his teeth, I'll need to make sure he has money for provisions." The man walked away, looking as if he'd aged a decade since last night. His shoulders drooped, and his head hung down.

Jared's heart hurt for him and for the whole Montgomery family. Thumping noises from over his head indicated Benjamin's continued anger.

The door to the library beckoned him, offering a quiet interlude. His heart heavy, Jared sought out its peace and the wisdom he knew he could glean from reading God's Word.

fourteen

Amelia met Tabitha downstairs, her dark cloak pulled tightly about her. It was well past midnight, and the rest of the household was slumbering peacefully. The day had been eventful, starting with Luke's promotion and her near exposure and ending with Benjamin's decision to join up.

"I don't know if I can leave you." Tabitha's wide eyes shone with tears.

Amelia hugged her and sniffed a little. "Don't be silly. Think how wonderful it will be to control your own life. You are going to be free the way God intended you to be. You and Melek will settle down in Canada and start a family of your own. After the war is over, Luke and I will come visit you." She handed Tabitha a small leather pouch. "This contains some money. It should help smooth your path and make sure you have something to get you started in your new life."

Tabitha nodded and placed the pouch inside the meager bag that held her most precious belongings. "I don't know how to thank you."

"You can thank me by leading a happy life." Amelia led the way to the door. She had memorized the instructions on the note Mrs. Downing had passed to her in the parlor. It had said to meet at the same location the lady had taken her to during the rally. The most perilous part of their journey would be avoiding Confederate patrols. They were to approach the church on foot and give the call of a mockingbird. Then they would be met by Melek and his current group of escaped slaves. Tabitha would go with him, and Amelia would return home.

Amelia wished they could use horses for the trek across town, but they would be less detectable on foot. It would take them an hour to walk across town in the dark—their progress would be slowed by having to avoid patrols.

They made their way down the dark streets, barely daring to speak for fear of being caught. Amelia had to stop from time to time and study the map that had been included with Mrs. Downing's instructions.

They were only a few blocks from the church when disaster struck. She turned a corner and nearly walked right into a mounted patrol. For a brief instant, she froze and her entire life seemed to flash in front of her eyes. Then Tabitha grabbed her elbow and pulled her into the recesses of a shadowy doorway. Amelia held her breath, trying to hear if they'd been seen. But neither of the men raised an alarm. They seemed to be half asleep as they walked their tired horses down the street, passing scant feet from where Tabitha and Amelia were hiding.

The two of them waited for several minutes before moving forward.

"That was close." Tabitha's whisper sounded loud in the quiet street.

Amelia placed a finger over her mouth and nodded. Then she gathered her courage and stepped out of the shadows, half expecting to hear a shout from one of the soldiers. No one, however, pursued them, and they made the rest of the trip without incident.

When Amelia recognized the rendezvous, she pointed it out to Tabitha. Then she tightened her lips and whistled.

After a moment, the hoot of an owl answered. A tall figure materialized out of the darkness. Melek.

They were safe. Tabitha fell into his arms with a cry of relief. Even in the dim light Amelia could see the tenderness on his dark face. It was a poignant moment for her—saying good-bye to her closest friend. But she could do no less. The hope they would see each other again in the future—on earth or definitely in heaven—would have to sustain her.

Melek looked over Tabitha's bowed head at her. "Thank you."

"Take good care of her."

"I will." He smiled down at Tabitha for a moment before returning his attention to Amelia. "Will you be okay by yourself?"

Amelia nodded. "I'll be fine."

"We need to get started, little flower."

Tabitha nodded against his shoulder. She pulled away from him and threw her arms around Amelia. "God bless you."

"He already has." She felt the words in her heart. Seeing the two of them together was a blessing. Their love was apparent in every glance, every gesture. It was so much deeper than what she felt for Luke. The thought hit her like a blow. The affection she felt toward Luke was a pale shadow of what Melek and Tabitha had. Was it enough to base a marriage upon?

The question seemed to chase her all the way back to her aunt and uncle's home. She didn't know what to do. Should she marry Luke and hope to develop the kind of love Tabitha and Melek had? Or should she end the betrothal and continue looking for the right man? And what about her parents? They would tell her she was being foolish to pine for romantic love. Luke was a good man. He would see to her needs. But was that enough?

The sky was lightening as she snuggled under the pile of quilts on her bed, but sleep still escaped her. She had no idea what to do. Amelia closed her eyes and prayed for guidance, unsure of exactly what answer she was seeking. Eventually peace settled over her, and she drifted into slumber.

❧

Early the next morning, Amelia was awakened by a pounding at her bedroom door.

Before she could answer, Aunt Laura pushed the door open and hurried in. She was dressed in a flowing wrapper, and the long plait of her hair was draped over her shoulder.

Amelia's heart skipped a beat. "What's wrong?"

"Have you seen Tabitha this morning?"

Amelia rubbed her eyes and tried to arrange her thoughts. She glanced about the room as if expecting Tabitha to appear in one of the corners. "No, why?"

Aunt Laura clasped her hands in a prayerful gesture. "It seems your slave has run away."

"Run away? Tabitha? Are you sure?" Amelia was proud of the confused tone in her voice. She ought to be an actress. "Perhaps she's gone on an errand and will be back in a little while."

Her aunt considered the suggestion then shook her head. "Someone would know if she'd been sent on an errand. No, I'm afraid she's escaped. You'll likely never see her again."

The poignancy of their good-byes came back to Amelia full force. "I hope she's safe."

"Safe? You hope she's safe? I wish that was my only concern. I don't know how we'll tell your parents that their valuable property has disappeared."

Amelia slid her toes out of the bed. "Don't worry about that. I'll tell Papa when I return home. Perhaps I'll say she ran away during our journey back to Nashville. That way he can't blame you at all."

A calculating look came over her aunt's face, but then she sighed. "No, we can't do that. It's not Christian to lie, even to protect one's self." She shook her head. "I'll send one of our slaves up to help you dress. Do you have a preference?"

"No." Amelia forced the word out. She could barely focus on her aunt's dithering for the truth the woman had just uttered. Lying, even to protect one's self, was not acceptable behavior for a Christian. She knew that, but somehow she'd forgotten it. She opened her mouth to confess her part in Tabitha's disappearance, but shouts from outside stopped her.

Amelia ran to the window to see what was going on. "It's Captain Talbot. I wonder why he's here."

Her aunt hurried over to where she stood. "You're not expecting your betrothed?"

Concern swept Amelia. "No. Something must have happened." She urged Aunt Laura out of the bedroom and made short work of her toilette. Her stays were not as tight as usual, her skirt felt slightly askew, and her hair was a mess, but she was downstairs at the door to the library in less than fifteen minutes.

She stood still for a moment to catch her breath and heard Luke's accusing voice, punctuated by her uncle's angry questions. She knocked briefly and entered, stopping all conversation.

Jared was sitting in his usual spot next to the window. Luke was leaning over him, his fist balled as though he wanted to beat the truth out of Jared. Uncle Francis was ensconced behind his desk, and she had never seen him looking so grave, even on the day Benjamin joined the army.

"What's going on in here?" Amelia walked over to Luke

and placed her hand on his arm. The muscles in it were as hard as granite. "Luke? What's wrong?"

He glared at her. "Treason."

Fear raked her spine. Amelia could almost feel the noose tightening around her throat. "What do you mean?"

"Someone in this household has been helping slaves escape."

This was even worse than she had imagined. "Why would you think such a thing?"

"We captured a runaway slave last night. Most of his group got away, but we did learn the identity of at least one of them." Luke's gaze clashed with hers once more. "Tabitha."

She could feel the blood draining from her cheeks. "Aunt L–Laura said she was missing, but I. . .I thought she was on an errand."

"Only if her errand is in Canada."

"Did you catch her, too?" She squeezed the question out of her tight throat.

"No."

Amelia sat down on the sofa with a thump. At least Tabitha had gotten away. A prayer of thanksgiving filled her. "I see."

"It's not your fault. Tabitha should have been grateful for her easy station." He turned and pointed a finger at Jared. "She would still be here if not for the Judas in your midst."

A glint caught her attention and Amelia gasped. A pair of handcuffs dangled from Luke's hand. "You're arresting Jared?"

Luke nodded. "Don't look so upset, Amelia. You should be congratulating me. Jared Stuart is the Mockingbird."

She sprang from the sofa and watched in horror as he fastened the cuffs around Jared's wrists. "This is absurd,

Luke. He cannot be the Mockingbird."

Luke's eyebrows rose. "I know you feel sympathy for Jared, but you needn't try to protect him. The man we caught told us the leader of the group was connected to this household. And Jared is the only one with abolitionist leanings."

Amelia knew his logic was faulty, but she couldn't tell Luke that without exposing herself. "It can't be Jared. It has to be someone else."

Uncle Francis put an arm around her shoulders. "There is no one else, dear."

She shook her head. "No." What could she do to stop Jared's arrest? Her mind couldn't come up with a plan. She had to do something, but she had no idea what.

Luke marched Jared out of the house as she watched helplessly. Everything was spiraling out of control—like an unstoppable spring flood.

"I know you're as shocked as I am." Uncle Francis shook his head slowly. "Remember, I'm the one who recently told my son he should be more like Jared."

Amelia wanted to run after the two men, but what would she say? If she confessed the truth, she would be arrested. And her guiltless relatives would face suspicion and disgrace. "Where is Luke taking him?"

"To the school. Our friend General Zollicoffer has already filled all the jails. It seems many traitors reside in our fair city."

But Amelia knew this time Luke had the wrong person. She was the *real* traitor. . .to Luke, to her parents, to her aunt and uncle, and now to Jared. But most importantly—and tragically—to God.

fifteen

The new maid assigned to her in Tabitha's absence smoothed Amelia's cloak over her shoulders. While they were waiting for the carriage to be brought around, Uncle Francis emerged from his study to discover where she was going. She mustered a bright smile and told him she had promised to make a morning visit to the Downing household. Another lie. Her conscience hammered her all the way to Mrs. Downing's home, but Amelia didn't know what else she could have done. Everything was in such a mess.

Mrs. Downing's butler, a grizzled black man with a pronounced limp, announced her. Amelia was relieved no other ladies were visiting this morning. Faye was sitting next to the fire, a basket of mending beside her. Mrs. Downing, seated on a horsehair sofa, wore a pale pink morning dress that was covered with bows and laces. Her outfit reminded Amelia of a profusion of azalea blossoms. She dropped a curtsy and nodded to Faye.

"Come in, dear, and tell us why you are about so early this morning." Mrs. Downing waved her to a nearby chair.

"A train accident occurred last night."

"I see." Mrs. Downing shook her head in warning before turning to her daughter. "Faye, would you go upstairs and fetch my wrap? I am feeling a little chilled."

Her daughter put down her mending. "Yes, Ma."

"And check in the kitchen for some of those tarts I like."

As soon as Faye was gone, her mother turned to Amelia. "Tell me what happened."

Amelia recounted the story Luke had told her and ended with Jared's arrest. "I cannot bear the thought of his spending even one night in jail for something he did not do."

Mrs. Downing stood up and walked to the fireplace. "I'm afraid it cannot be helped."

"Yes, it can. I can tell them who the real Mockingbird is. I am tired of all the subterfuge anyway, and I've been having serious doubts about whether I'm following the Lord's will in all of this."

The older lady sat down again, an intense look on her face. "Think of all the poor souls who may lose their freedom if you step forward now. We have only recently begun to see success with our work, and a lot of it is due to your efforts. You cannot quit now."

"The railroad will continue without me. That is its strength. The loss of a single agent may cause some hardship, but it will not be shut down."

"Consider this, Amelia. Your friend, Jared, is a known abolitionist, right?"

Amelia nodded.

"Then he probably doesn't mind spending some time in jail. He might even be glad to be imprisoned if it means the real Mockingbird can continue working."

The argument was tempting. It would be so easy to simply remain silent. "But I cannot continue to lie. To tell you the truth, I am almost looking forward to confessing."

Mrs. Downing tapped her chin with one finger as she considered Amelia's words. "At least wait a few days until things quiet down. Give me time to find someone to take your place."

Faye reentered the parlor at that point and their conversation halted. As the three women discussed the latest news, part of Amelia's mind considered her hostess's request.

She took her leave of Mrs. Downing and Faye and climbed back into the carriage, having decided to honor Mrs. Downing's request. Halfway home, however, she changed her mind. She could not remain quiet. Not even one more minute. Jared could not suffer for her transgressions.

❧

Jared looked around the empty room in West College that had once housed his fellow students. How carefree those days seemed. In the two months since the closing of the school, everything had changed. He supposed he should have returned to his parents' home in Nashville, but he could not bring himself to regret the time he'd spent here, even though it had led to his imprisonment. A temporary condition—or so he hoped. Once they found the real Mockingbird, Luke Talbot would have to release him.

He briefly considered offering to help Talbot in his search for the Mockingbird, but then he dismissed the idea. He might not agree with the lies and deceit involved in keeping the Underground Railroad in operation, but he could not fault the men and women who used it to escape the tyranny of slavery.

The kernel of an idea formed in his mind for a new article. He could write about the railroad. But what new slant could he give it?

As he was considering possibilities, one of the guards came and unlocked the door to his room. "Captain Talbot wants to see you."

Jared searched the soldier's face for any hint of what was going on. He looked to be in his midtwenties. His uniform was well worn and bore the evidence of several patches, but it was worn with evident pride. He gestured toward the hallway with his chin.

Jared nodded and preceded him. The hallway was filled with the moans and groans of the wounded soldiers who were housed here. Jared's heart hurt for them. So much pain.

They climbed the steps to what used to be the president's office and entered the room. He was not surprised to see Captain Talbot sitting behind the president's desk, but the other occupant in the room made him halt in his tracks. What was Amelia doing here?

"Sit down, Stuart."

Jared sat down in the wooden chair facing the desk. He glanced at Amelia out of the corner of his eye. Had she been crying? She looked pale and her eyes were red.

"I have a couple of questions for you."

"What is she doing here?"

"Never mind that."

Jared bit his lip to keep from responding. It wouldn't do his situation much good to antagonize the captain.

"You have some loyal friends in Knoxville who insist you are a man of your word. Is that true?"

Jared nodded slowly. "My parents raised me to believe that honesty is of paramount importance."

Luke leaned forward and stared directly into his eyes. "Then I ask you to give me your word that you are not working with the Underground Railroad and that you are not the agent called the Mockingbird."

Knowing he had nothing to be ashamed of, Jared held the captain's gaze as he answered. "I am not, nor have I ever been, involved with the Underground Railroad. Nor have I ever been known by the name Mockingbird. The very idea is ludicrous. I use words, not lies, to fight injustice."

"You see?" Amelia spoke for the first time. "It's as I've said. Jared is innocent. If you want to arrest someone, you know who it must be."

Jared could feel his brows drawing together. What was she talking about? Who should be arrested?

Luke's chair scraped the floor as he pushed himself away from the desk. "I suppose you're right."

Amelia stood as he approached her and held her hands out. A roaring sound enveloped Jared as he watched Luke fasten handcuffs around her dainty wrists.

"I'm so sorry, Jared."

Their gazes met, and the truth slammed into him. Amelia Montgomery was the Mockingbird.

Jared was speechless. How had she done it? And why? Why hadn't she come to him? She must have lied over and over again, deceiving all of them. He slumped back in his chair.

"You'll let him leave?" Her voice was drained of emotion. Her whole attitude was one of resignation.

Jared wanted to be angry with her, but it was impossible. How could he maintain anger when she was sacrificing her freedom for his own?

"Yes, but that is the least thing that should concern you now." Luke's face was frozen as if to hide his pain.

Jared felt an unwelcome empathy with the man. Amelia had betrayed both of them.

Luke turned away from her and approached Jared's chair, a master key in his hands. He unlocked the shackles and waited until Jared stood up. "You may have escaped justice this time, but you'd better watch your step."

Jared was glad to be exonerated, but at what price?

His gaze lingered on Amelia's bowed head and slumping shoulders. "What will happen to her?"

"That will be up to the general." Luke's harsh tone took Jared's attention from Amelia.

"You can stop her from being. . .executed, can't you?" He stole another glance at her and saw a tear drip from her chin and land on her shackled hands. His heart broke. Jared took a step toward her, wanting to comfort her.

Luke stepped between them. "Stay away from her. You've done enough harm."

"Don't blame Jared." Amelia's voice was thick with her tears. "What I did has nothing to do with him."

"You have to protect her." Jared adjusted his spectacles so he could see Luke more clearly. "She is your betrothed."

"That's right. Her fate is in my hands." Luke's mouth twisted into a sneer. "Not yours. You should escape while you have the chance, before I change my mind and have you arrested for fomenting rebellion in the Montgomery household. If you hadn't filled Amelia's head with your unrealistic notions, she probably wouldn't be here right now."

"It's not his fault." Amelia raised her head, and Jared saw the streaks her tears had left on her cheeks.

"Is that so?" Luke's dark gaze raked both of them. "You're not the same girl I grew up with. And don't think I haven't seen the closeness between the two of you."

Jared wanted to dispute the angry man, but he couldn't come up with any words. He watched as Amelia was taken away by the same soldier who'd escorted him.

Heartbroken, he shook his head at Luke and stumbled from the room. He made his way across the campus by instinct. A part of his brain noticed the differences since the soldiers had taken over the school. Long, deep trenches defaced the hillside sloping to the river, and military tents had sprung up like mushrooms after a spring rain. Soldiers milled about, but no one seemed to pay much attention to him.

Where should he go? What should he do? Jared had no idea. He buried his hands in his pockets and wandered the streets of Knoxville, feeling like a rudderless boat tossed by high waves.

How could he have missed the evidence? He was supposed to be a reporter. He was supposed to be aware of what was happening around him. How had Amelia managed to hide her double life from him?

Jared thought back over the past months. Had he been blinded by her beauty? The answer was a resounding yes. He felt like he'd been an idiot. He ought to feel betrayed, but he could not summon up that emotion. Not when her goal had been freedom for slaves. And when it really counted, she had dropped her subterfuge and come forward to free him. What would happen to her now? A shudder passed through him, but it was not caused by the cold winter air.

He could not leave Amelia imprisoned, but what could he do? He considered going to her aunt and uncle, but that would mean he'd have to confess what their niece had done. He didn't want to do that. They should get that information directly from Amelia.

If this had happened a few days earlier, he could have enlisted Benjamin's help. He thought of the scrapes his friend had dragged him through. But those days were behind them. Benjamin was a soldier, and his superiors would not look kindly on his helping a confessed traitor.

If only his father were here. Adam Stuart would know exactly how to handle the situation without resorting to illegal schemes or outlandish ploys. Thinking of his father made Jared realize what must be done. He needed to secure Amelia's freedom and leave Knoxville. It was time to go home. In Nashville, he would find wiser counsel. Perhaps he could convince Luke to release Amelia into his custody or at least talk Luke into taking her back to her parents' remote plantation home where she would be kept far from involvement with runaway slaves and the Underground Railroad.

Unaware of his surroundings, Jared stumbled on a rock. He would have fallen but caught hold of the rough brick exterior of an empty building. He looked around and recognized the area. He was only a block from Mr. Stone's home—the current office of the *Tennessee Tribune*. He thanked God for leading him to the very place he needed to be. Telling Mr. Stone about his plans to leave was the first step in breaking ties with Knoxville, and his employer would have to find another reporter to write articles for *The Voice of Reason*.

With a new sense of purpose, Jared strode to the house and knocked on Mr. Stone's door. He was ushered into the living room, where he stood in front of the welcome warmth of a roaring fire. He spread his hands out and sighed slightly as they began to thaw out. The door opened, and he turned to greet the man who had hired him.

A smile creased Mr. Stone's face as he entered the room. "This is an unexpected pleasure, Mr. Stuart. Have you come on business? I have already received your latest piece. It's excellent as always. Your talent grows stronger with each article you produce."

Pleasure warmed Jared's heart. On a day so filled with difficulties, the complimentary words were a balm to his soul. "Thank you, sir. You don't know how much it means to me to hear you say so."

"Do you have another article for me? Or is there some other reason you dropped by?"

Jared pushed his spectacles up. "I don't have a new article. In fact, that's sort of the reason I'm here." He stopped and blew out a puff of air. "I mean to say I've decided to go back home, so I won't be able to continue writing for *The Voice of Reason*."

"I see." Mr. Stone sat down on a convenient chair. He stared at the dancing flames in the fireplace before turning back to face Jared. "I cannot say I am surprised. I have been expecting something of the sort since your school term ended. Young men must always throw their energy into fighting."

"I don't know about that." Jared walked to the window and looked out. The pale winter sun, almost completely obscured by lowering clouds, had barely passed its zenith. What was Amelia doing right now? Was she sitting in the same room he had occupied before Luke released him? Was she frightened? Cold? His heart seemed to absorb some of the chill from the other side of the window. "I. . .something has come up that demands my attention."

"I hope it's not bad news?" Mr. Stone's voice invited Jared to expound.

He didn't yet feel he could bare his soul about the events of the morning. The pain was still too fresh. "No. I trust my abrupt departure won't inconvenience you."

Mr. Stone pushed himself up from his chair and came to stand next to Jared at the window. "Don't worry about me. It's been a pleasure to watch you grow as a writer. God has given you a great talent, and I'm sure He will lead you on to loftier heights."

Jared thanked the man before taking his leave. It had been

reassuring to hear Mr. Stone's confidence in him and to be reminded that God had not deserted him. . .or Amelia. A plan began to form in his mind, and he strode through the streets of Knoxville with renewed determination. He knew exactly how to unlock the bars of Amelia's prison.

❧

It was nearly two o'clock by the time Jared made his way back to his former campus. He talked the sentry into letting him pass and made his way to the place where he'd last seen Luke, praying that the man would still be there.

"Come in." Luke's voice answered his knock.

Jared sent a wordless plea to God before entering the room. He would need the Lord's help if he was to succeed.

Luke was sitting behind his desk, a stack of papers in front of him. He looked up as Jared entered, and his features registered his surprise. "What are you doing here? I thought I'd seen the last of you."

Jared ignored the question. "You love her, don't you?" He watched the other man's eyes closely. There it was. Pain. And fear. Luke was afraid Amelia didn't love him. That was the answer. It gave Jared the bargaining chip he needed. "Of course you love her. You asked her to be your wife."

"I don't see what my feelings have to do with anything. Amelia has committed some very serious crimes that would bring imprisonment even if we were not at war."

"What if I promise never to see Amelia again?"

A frown brought Luke's eyebrows together. "How will that change things?"

At least the man was curious. It gave Jared the courage to continue. "You suspect Amelia and I have feelings for each other. I cannot vouch for her, but I can tell you that I love her. Even after learning how she has deceived me, I cannot find it in my heart to condemn her actions. She was trying to help people who needed her."

"She has confessed to treason."

Jared refused to be deterred by the man's cold tone. "I know you love Amelia, too. As your wife, she would be protected from the consequences of her actions. You are probably right that my influence is what led her to rebellion. I will return to Nashville immediately. I can board the next train out of Knoxville and leave this part of Tennessee for good. You won't have to wonder if Amelia is being influenced by me or my feelings for her. I will never contact her again. Once I'm gone, she will be totally committed to her marriage to you. She'll be more interested in setting up her household than altruism."

"What if she doesn't agree?"

Jared sighed. "It's up to you to convince her. I know she cares for you or she never would have agreed to marry you. Amelia somehow got caught up in working for the Underground Railroad. But you saw her a little while ago. Her remorse was obvious. She knows she's hurt those who care about her. She will listen to reason."

Luke took a turn around the office as he considered the proposal. Jared saw his expression move from despair to hope, from confusion to certainty. Finally the man walked over to him and thrust out his hand. "I have your word on this?"

What other choice did he have? He would do everything possible to protect Amelia. Jared's heart would not let him do any less. He shook Luke's hand. He would gladly pay the price of giving her up—knowing he would never see her again—to free the woman he loved.

sixteen

The guard had left Amelia in a large room cluttered with chairs and desks that must have been removed to make space for the rows of wounded soldiers lying on cots in the former classrooms. She wondered if it was the same room that had held Jared.

She took a handkerchief from her reticule and blew her nose. No more tears, no more weakness. Even if the general decided to execute her. She was not proud of the pain she'd caused, but she was glad to have been a part of setting Tabitha and the others free.

A knock on the door interrupted her thoughts. She glanced at the untouched tray of food a soldier had brought her earlier. She'd not been able to swallow a single morsel. Her stomach was too unsettled, and her throat still seemed full of tears. Even the smell of the roasted chicken made her feel queasy. It would be a relief to have it removed. "Come in."

Luke's broad shoulders filled the doorway. Why was he seeking her out? He'd been so angry once she convinced him of the truth.

Then his purpose dawned on her. "I suppose you came for your ring." Amelia fumbled with the golden band.

"No." He stepped into the room and closed the door behind him. "I'm not ready to release you from your promise."

"But won't it hurt your career when the truth is known?"

"Your friend, Jared, has proposed a solution."

Amelia's heart doubled its speed. Jared had argued on her behalf? "I thought both of you were scandalized by what I've done."

"Both of us have strong feelings when it comes to you, Amelia. And we have reason to be disappointed with your choice to deceive both of us, but it's time to move beyond what's past and make plans about what has to be done next."

So this was it. Amelia wondered if she would be hanged for her involvement with the Underground Railroad. She prayed for the fortitude to face her death with equanimity. After all, her own decisions were what had brought her to this.

Luke cleared his throat to get her attention. "I can't say that I blame Jared for falling in love with you, but at least he has the sense to put your safety above his feelings." He leaned against the door and watched her.

"Jared loves me?" As soon as the words slipped out, she gasped. Even she could hear the longing in her voice.

Luke's face changed. His eyes darkened and his mouth twisted. "Honesty? Do you have to be so transparent now? What happened to the woman who lied to everyone for her own reasons?"

"I'm sorry, Luke." She twisted the engagement ring off her finger and held it out to him.

"I could keep you here, you know."

"I'm resigned to stay for the duration of the war if that's what you decide."

"Please don't do this, Amelia. Don't throw away what we have. We can still have a life together."

She shook her head and looked down at the ring still in her hand. "I didn't mean to hurt you, Luke. I love you like a brother."

"I see." He took the ring but then caught her wrists in his hands. "My feelings are strong enough for both of us. Won't you reconsider? I'm sure I can make you happy."

She pulled her hands free and took a step back. "You're a wonderful man, Luke, and you deserve a wife who returns your feelings."

Luke's shoulders slumped. "Would it make any difference if I told you Jared has promised to have nothing more to do with you?"

Amelia closed her eyes as the words burned through her like poison. In that instant she knew the truth. She loved Jared. Not with the tepid feeling of friendship she felt for the man in front of her. She loved Jared Stuart with her whole heart, and she always would. That was why her betrothal to Luke had felt more like a cage than a promise. It was sheer willpower that kept her from sinking to her knees. "I told you Jared had nothing to do with the Mockingbird." She forced the words through clenched teeth.

"He'll soon be on his way back to Nashville."

Amelia tried to force her lips into a pleasant smile, but her muscles betrayed her. She looked into Luke's dark eyes, unable to say anything.

"I hope one day to find a woman who cares as much for me." The muscles in his face tightened, dragging his mouth downward. "But it is evident to me you are not that woman, Amelia. Everything you said to me and Jared this afternoon will remain between the three of us, so I have no reason to hold you any longer."

"You're letting me go?" Her eyes stung with unshed tears. Regret filled her heart. Luke deserved so much more than she could ever offer him.

"Who would really believe that you, a gently bred heiress,

are the Mockingbird?" His laughter had a sardonic ring. "But I must have a promise from you."

Was he going to tell her to stay away from Jared? She could not make that promise. Not now that she knew the truth of her feelings for him.

"You must never tell anyone else the truth about the Mockingbird, or I will be blamed for abetting a criminal."

Her eyes searched his. "You have my word, Luke."

"Good. Then you are free to leave. I've ordered a carriage to return you to your aunt and uncle's home. I hope you will have the good sense to stay away from the abolitionists in town. I don't ever want to repeat this day's events."

"Thank you, Luke." She reached up and placed a chaste kiss on his cheek. "You're a good friend." Amelia followed him to the front door and allowed him to help her into the carriage. "I'll never forget this."

"Be happy, Amelia." He closed the carriage door with a soft click. "God bless you."

&

Cold rain pelted the roof of her carriage, and Amelia wondered if it would turn into sleet. Her heart went out to the poor soldiers like Cousin Benjamin who likely had little shelter from the weather.

She watched anxiously as the driver guided the conveyance through the streets to her aunt and uncle's home. Was the trip taking longer than normal? Or was it her anxiety that lengthened the distance?

Finally the driver pulled up the horses, and she saw the familiar front door. Her foot tapped a rapid beat as she waited for him to let down the steps so she could disembark. She barely noticed the umbrella he held above her head as she hurried out of the carriage and up the steps to the front door, but she did have the presence of mind to thank the man before disappearing into the hallway.

Amelia hurried to the parlor, wondering how Uncle Francis and Aunt Laura had received Jared when he returned home. Had they been suspicious of him? Or had they been relieved to learn he was not the Mockingbird. And what had he told them about her disappearance?

She pasted a wobbly smile on her lips as she pushed the door open. Part of her was anxious to confront Jared about his feelings, but another part of her dreaded having to face him since he'd found out about her work with the Underground Railroad. Would he be cold? Or had he forgiven her? There was only one way to find out for sure. She took a deep breath and stepped inside the room.

Aunt Laura was sitting in her favorite chair on the right side of the hearth, her needlework in her lap. She jumped up, heedless of the sampler's falling to the floor. "Oh, there you are. We were really beginning to worry."

Uncle Francis was ensconced in the chair on the opposite side of the fireplace and held a book, which he closed abruptly as he looked up. "We wondered where you were, niece."

Amelia bent to kiss her aunt and then turned to her uncle. "I apologize. I was unavoidably detained and didn't think to send you a note."

"After the unpleasantness this morning, I told your uncle you had probably sought out your betrothed to ask for his help in recovering your slave." Aunt Laura nodded and settled back into her chair, retrieving her sampler and once again plying her needle with speed and accuracy.

"Speaking of notes, we did receive one from the Stuart boy." Uncle Francis snorted. "Your aunt and I went to

Benjamin's encampment north of town earlier today to make certain he had everything he needed. When we got back, we were informed Jared had slunk in here during our absence and left a note thanking us for our hospitality. His note also claimed he'd been exonerated of the charge of treason. Said he had nothing to do with that Mockingbird fellow who's been helping slaves escape."

Amelia wanted to ask where Jared was now, but Aunt Laura interrupted her husband's dialogue. "Speaking of slaves, did you find Tabitha?"

"No." Amelia sat down on the sofa across from her aunt and uncle and twisted her hands in her lap. "I. . .I have a confession to make about Tabitha." She took a deep breath to steady herself before continuing. "I'm the one who helped Tabitha escape."

"You what!" Uncle Francis dropped his book.

Amelia cringed at the angry tone but would not let her gaze fall from his shocked one. "I'm sorry. I didn't mean to cause so much trouble. My. . .Tabitha has fallen in love, and I wanted her to be happy."

"Have you lost your senses?" Aunt Laura asked. "Her freedom was not yours to give."

"Tabitha is more like a sister to me than a slave." Amelia raised her chin. "I could not bear to see her unhappy."

"I don't know what this world is coming to." Uncle Francis sounded more puzzled than angry. He shook his head. "Your father is going to be very disappointed that you freed his property."

A rueful smile bent her lips upward. "You're right, but I hope he will eventually forgive me."

After folding her needlework and placing it in her basket, Aunt Laura moved to the sofa. "Of course he will forgive you.

He loves you, Amelia. You are his daughter." She put an arm around Amelia and hugged her close.

Uncle Francis rolled his eyes. "Yes, yes. My brother may be hardheaded, but he will forgive you once you settle down and start providing him with grandchildren." He pointed a finger at her. "He's bound to be pleased with your engagement. Luke Talbot is a fine man."

"Yes, well, that's another thing I have to tell you about."

"What's wrong?" Aunt Laura pulled back a little and looked at her.

"Luke and I have decided we will not suit." Amelia told them about her interview with Luke and how she had confessed to helping Tabitha get away, but she avoided mentioning the Mockingbird, in deference to her promise to Luke.

"I'm sure your young man will reconsider his decision once he has time to cool off." Aunt Laura patted her hand.

"He must have been shocked by your confession," her uncle agreed. "And also embarrassed to have to set Jared free. But he'll probably change his mind once he catches the real culprit."

It was time to change the subject and broach the question she most wanted answered. "Did Jared's note say when he would return?"

Aunt Laura frowned at her. "Return? I thought you understood. Jared is gone. He is probably already on his way back to Nashville."

"His note said he wants to do his part to end the war." Uncle Francis shook his head. "Who knows what that means?"

The words echoed through Amelia. Who indeed? Certainly not her. She didn't know why she'd expected him to be here, anyway. Luke had told her about Jared's promise.

One of the things she admired about Jared was his integrity. He would not linger here, knowing she would be coming back before too long.

All her hopes of being reunited with him died. It was too late.

One of the slaves came in to announce dinner, but Amelia knew she could not eat a single morsel. With a mumbled excuse, she went upstairs to her bedroom. Heartbroken, she threw herself across her bed and wept bitterly into the softness of her pillow. A maid came in, but she waved her away. She was too distraught to change into her nightgown. Who cared about such mundane things when her whole world had fallen apart?

Nothing penetrated her grief until the soft sounds of a birdcall drew her head from the pillow. She glanced toward the corner of her bedroom at her mockingbird trapped in its ornate cage. She pushed herself up from the bed and wandered toward it, her bruised heart somehow lightened by the lovely sounds it was producing. Their sweetness seemed like a promise from God.

Her breath caught as an idea took form. "I know just what we need to do so we can both be free, my friend." She moved to her dresser and picked up the mockingbird brooch Jared had given her. It was the first thing she put into her valise, followed by hastily folded clothing. Hoping she had packed enough necessities, Amelia changed into her nightgown and slipped between the covers. She would need a good night's sleep if she was going to rise at first light.

seventeen

The sun was beginning to push back the ebony texture of the night sky when Amelia arrived at the train station. She could barely contain her anticipation as the coachmen assisted her from the carriage. She only hoped she had guessed correctly that Jared would make the return journey by train.

The busy station had changed considerably in the months since her arrival. The civilian crowds had disappeared, replaced by young men in gray uniforms who guarded crated supplies with weary eyes. The ticket window was deserted, so she asked one of the passing soldiers where she could board the train to Nashville.

He raised an arm and pointed to a long line of boxcars. "The conductor should be able to help you."

Amelia thanked him and turned to the train. She looked for Jared's familiar face among the men she passed, her heart threatening to burst from her chest. She had almost reached the metal steps when a shrill whistle sounded and the cars began to move.

She gasped. The train was leaving! She had to get on board! Her future depended on it.

The train began picking up speed. Without a thought to her dignity, Amelia raised her skirts and ran forward. But it was no use. She was too late. Jared had left Knoxville without her.

❧

Jared slumped in his seat and tried to convince himself it

was right to leave Knoxville. He had spent a restless night at a nearby boardinghouse, his mind plagued with grief and doubt. He was looking forward to seeing his family, of course. Missing them had been the hardest part of going to school so far away. But he was leaving a large part of his heart here.

To be more specific, he was leaving a big portion of it in Amelia's hands. And the ironic thing was she had no idea. She would marry Captain Luke Talbot and start a family. Maybe one day, some year in the far future, he would run into her on the streets of Nashville, a brood of young children in her wake.

He shook his head to empty it of the depressing picture and looked out the window as the train pulled from the station. His eyes slowly adjusted to the darkness as the train began to gather speed. He pushed his spectacles up and looked around, noticing only a couple of other passengers sitting on nearby benches—a far cry from the dozens who had traveled north only a few short months ago.

The war was changing everything. Now the trains were needed to move troops and supplies from battlefield to battlefield, and few private parties were on board. Of course most people didn't want to be traveling in such difficult times, either. Jared had been warned by the stationmaster that the train might not get all the way to Chattanooga, much less to Nashville. The destruction of tracks and bridges was growing more common each day, and it was becoming harder for the Confederacy to replace damaged rails and crossties.

The car lurched suddenly and Jared barely managed to keep himself on the narrow bench seat as the train halted. Three gray-uniformed soldiers ran through the car toward the engine, their rifles pointing forward. What was going on?

Had the train been attacked? Jared looked outside, but he could see nothing wrong.

"Can you hear anything?" One of the men he'd seen earlier pushed himself into the aisle.

Jared shook his head. "No. Maybe it's only livestock."

"More likely to be destroyed tracks," said one of the other passengers.

The man who was standing pointed his finger in the direction the soldiers had gone. "They're coming back." He slipped back into his seat.

Jared could hear the soldiers now. His shoulder relaxed as he heard them laughing at something. The problem must be minor. Perhaps they would soon be on their way.

A pair of soldiers opened the door and ushered in a woman who was holding a birdcage aloft in one hand.

Jared's eyes widened as he recognized the wheat-gold color of the woman's hair. His heart skipped a beat. "Amelia?"

"There he is." She pointed at him.

What was going on? He pushed himself to his feet. "What are you doing here?"

One of the soldiers clapped him on the shoulder. "You're a lucky fellow. Miss Montgomery here stopped the train by running her carriage across the tracks. She says she couldn't let you leave her behind in Knoxville."

Jared could do nothing but stare at Amelia as the soldiers continued on their way through the car.

"Can you forgive me?" She set her birdcage on one of the empty benches and stepped toward him.

Forgive her? He'd forgiven her almost instantly. In fact, while he could not condone her methods, he found himself impressed at the way she'd put her own safety aside to help slaves escape. "I think you're the bravest woman I've ever met."

"I'm not brave at all. I never intended to get involved with the Underground Railroad, but how could I ignore their plight?" She glanced up at him, her wide blue eyes swimming with tears. "But I hated deceiving my family. . .and you."

Jared cleared his throat. This was madness. He had promised Luke to have nothing to do with Amelia. Yet here they stood. He turned from her. "You should not be here."

A soft sound of distress answered his words.

Jared spun back to Amelia. "I'm sorry, but I made a promise to Luke."

Amelia's hurt look changed to hope, and she shook her head. "But you don't understand, Jared. Luke has released you from your promise. I am here with his blessing." She stepped closer and put a hand on his arm.

The words rolled around in his head for a moment before their meaning became clear. The love and tenderness in her expression made him feel like he was flying. The train lurched forward, and Jared quickly put an arm around Amelia to keep her from falling. Or maybe it was to keep himself from floating through the roof.

He could hardly believe it. He had lost all hope, but God had provided a way for them to be together. The sorrow that had filled him since boarding the train transformed into thankfulness, peace, and joy.

The forgotten cage behind her rocked slightly with the movement of the train, and its occupant began to chirp.

"Why did you bring the mockingbird with you?"

She glanced up at him, her face only inches from his. "I'm going to release him as soon as spring comes." Her voice was barely above a whisper. "How could I let my poor bird remain caged when my imprisoned heart has been set free?"

Jared looked down at Amelia, transfixed by the smile on her face. Heedless of the other passengers, he leaned forward and pressed a gentle kiss on her lips.

Love rushed through him as she put her arms around his neck. She was a special blessing, one he did not deserve. But Jared wasn't going to argue with God for giving him the opportunity to create a life with Amelia as his bride. On the contrary, he knew he would spend the rest of his life thanking God for removing the obstacles between them.

Jared kept his arm around her as he drew her to an empty seat. "I love you, Amelia."

"I love you, too, Jared. I couldn't bear the thought of a life without you."

"It won't be easy." He dropped a kiss behind her right ear. "I got a letter from Pa yesterday. He's been working with a group of state senators who opposed secession, and he wants me to join them."

"Will you have to fight with the army?"

Jared shook his head. "I cannot take up arms against other Tennesseans. Yet I cannot fight with those who would continue the institution of slavery. Pa is working with both sides to try to find a solution that will end the fighting. He's read some of my articles, and he thinks I may be able to sway some of those whose minds are closed."

"Your articles?" A look of satisfaction crossed her beautiful face. "I knew it. I knew you wrote those articles in *The Voice of Reason*. They were so well written, and the tenor of them reminded me of the piece you wrote for your literary society."

His cheeks reddened in a mixture of surprise and pleasure. "I'm glad you liked them."

"How could I not when the author has held my heart for so long in his grasp?"

Another thrill passed through him at her words. The song in his heart would undoubtedly rival the most beautiful call of any mockingbird.

A Letter To Our Readers

Dear Reader:

In order that we might better contribute to your reading enjoyment, we would appreciate your taking a few minutes to respond to the following questions. We welcome your comments and read each form and letter we receive. When completed, please return to the following:

Fiction Editor
Heartsong Presents
PO Box 719
Uhrichsville, Ohio 44683

1. Did you enjoy reading *The Mockingbird's Call* by Diane Ashley and Aaron McCarver?
   ❏ Very much! I would like to see more books by this author!
   ❏ Moderately. I would have enjoyed it more if

   _____

   _____

   _____

2. Are you a member of **Heartsong Presents**? ❏ Yes ❏ No
   If no, where did you purchase this book? _____

   _____

3. How would you rate, on a scale from 1 (poor) to 5 (superior), the cover design? _____

4. On a scale from 1 (poor) to 10 (superior), please rate the following elements.

   ____ Heroine   ____ Plot
   ____ Hero   ____ Inspirational theme
   ____ Setting   ____ Secondary characters

5. These characters were special because? _____
_____
_____

6. How has this book inspired your life? _____
_____
_____

7. What settings would you like to see covered in future
   Heartsong Presents books? _____
_____
_____

8. What are some inspirational themes you would like to see
   treated in future books? _____
_____
_____

9. Would you be interested in reading other **Heartsong
   Presents** titles? ❑ Yes ❑ No

10. Please check your age range:
    ❑ Under 18   ❑ 18-24
    ❑ 25-34   ❑ 35-45
    ❑ 46-55   ❑ Over 55

Name _____
Occupation _____
Address _____
City, State, Zip_____
E-mail _____

Presents

___HP792	*Sweet Forever*, R. Cecil	___HP847	*A Girl Like That*, F. Devine
___HP795	*A Treasure Reborn*, P. Griffin	___HP848	*Remembrance*, J. Spaeth
___HP796	*The Captain's Wife*, M. Davis	___HP851	*Straight for the Heart*, V. McDonough
___HP799	*Sandhill Dreams*, C. C. Putman	___HP852	*A Love All Her Own*, J. L. Barton
___HP800	*Return to Love*, S. P. Davis	___HP855	*Beacon of Love*, D. Franklin
___HP803	*Quills and Promises*, A. Miller	___HP856	*A Promise Kept*, C. C. Putman
___HP804	*Reckless Rogue*, M. Davis	___HP859	*The Master's Match*, T. H. Murray
___HP807	*The Greatest Find*, P. W. Dooly	___HP860	*Under the Tulip Poplar*, D. Ashley & A. McCarver
___HP808	*The Long Road Home*, R. Druten		
___HP811	*A New Joy*, S.P. Davis	___HP863	*All that Glitters*, L. Sowell
___HP812	*Everlasting Promise*, R.K. Cecil	___HP864	*Picture Bride*, Y. Lehman
___HP815	*A Treasure Regained*, P. Griffin	___HP867	*Hearts and Harvest*, A. Stockton
___HP816	*Wild at Heart*, V. McDonough	___HP868	*A Love to Cherish*, J. L. Barton
___HP819	*Captive Dreams*, C. C. Putman	___HP871	*Once a Thief*, F. Devine
___HP820	*Carousel Dreams*, P. W. Dooly	___HP872	*Kind-Hearted Woman*, J. Spaeth
___HP823	*Deceptive Promises*, A. Miller	___HP875	*The Bartered Bride*, E. Vetsch
___HP824	*Alias, Mary Smith*, R. Druten	___HP876	*A Promise Born*, C.C. Putman
___HP827	*Abiding Peace*, S. P. Davis	___HP877	*A Still, Small Voice*, K. O'Brien
___HP828	*A Season for Grace*, T. Bateman	___HP878	*Opie's Challenge*, T. Fowler
___HP831	*Outlaw Heart*, V. McDonough	___HP879	*A Bouquet for Iris*, D. Ashley & A. McCarver
___HP832	*Charity's Heart*, R. K. Cecil		
___HP835	*A Treasure Revealed*, P. Griffin	___HP880	*The Glassblower*, L.A. Eakes
___HP836	*A Love for Keeps*, J. L. Barton	___HP883	*Patterns and Progress*, A. Stockton
___HP839	*Out of the Ashes*, R. Druten	___HP884	*Love From Ashes*, Y. Lehman
___HP840	*The Petticoat Doctor*, P. W. Dooly	___HP887	*The Marriage Masquerade*, E. Vetsch
___HP843	*Copper and Candles*, A. Stockton	___HP888	*In Search of a Memory*, P. Griffin
___HP844	*Aloha Love*, Y. Lehman		

Great Inspirational Romance at a Great Price!

Heartsong Presents books are inspirational romances in contemporary and historical settings, designed to give you an enjoyable, spirit-lifting reading experience. You can choose wonderfully written titles from some of today's best authors like Wanda E. Brunstetter, Mary Connealy, Susan Page Davis, Cathy Marie Hake, Joyce Livingston, and many others.

When ordering quantities less than twelve, above titles are $2.97 each.
Not all titles may be available at time of order.

SEND TO: **Heartsong Presents** Readers' Service
P.O. Box 721, Uhrichsville, Ohio 44683

Please send me the items checked above. I am enclosing $ _____
(please add $4.00 to cover postage per order. OH add 7% tax. WA add 8.5%). Send check or money order, no cash or C.O.D.s, please.
To place a credit card order, call 1-740-922-7280.

NAME _____

ADDRESS _____

CITY/STATE _____ ZIP_____

HEARTSONG
PRESENTS

If you love Christian romance...

$10.99

You'll love Heartsong Presents' inspiring and faith-filled romances by today's very best Christian authors...Wanda E. Brunstetter, Mary Connealy, Susan Page Davis, Cathy Marie Hake, and Joyce Livingston, to mention a few!

When you join Heartsong Presents, you'll enjoy four brand-new, mass-market, 176-page books—two contemporary and two historical—that will build you up in your faith when you discover God's role in every relationship you read about!

Mass Market 176 Pages

Imagine...four new romances every four weeks—with men and women like you who long to meet the one God has chosen as the love of their lives...all for the low price of $10.99 postpaid.

To join, simply visit www.heartsong presents.com or complete the coupon below and mail it to the address provided.

✂ -

YES! Sign me up for Heartsong!

NEW MEMBERSHIPS WILL BE SHIPPED IMMEDIATELY!
Send no money now. We'll bill you only $10.99 postpaid with your first shipment of four books. Or for faster action, call 1-740-922-7280.

NAME _____

ADDRESS_____

CITY_____ STATE _____ ZIP _____

MAIL TO: HEARTSONG PRESENTS, P.O. Box 721, Uhrichsville, Ohio 44683
or sign up at WWW.HEARTSONGPRESENTS.COM